PENGUIN BOOKS

901

A VOYAGE TO PURILIA

ELMER RICE

ELMER RICE

A VOYAGE TO PURILIA

PENGUIN BOOKS

MELBOURNE · LONDON · BALTIMORE

First published August 1930
Published in Penguin Books 1954

Made and printed in Great Britain
for Penguin Books Ltd
Harmondsworth, Middlesex
by Hunt, Barnard & Co. Ltd, Aylesbury, Bucks

CHAPTER 1

WE had planned to take off shortly after daybreak, on the first day of May. At DeWitt Johnson's insistence, I spent the preceding night in a small hotel near the flying-field, but, although I went through the formality of removing my clothes and getting into bed, sleep was out of the question. The imminence of our departure, after so many weary months of preparation, produced in me a state of frenzied excitement; and my overwrought brain teemed with anticipations, conjectures, speculations, and – it must be confessed – fears. I was up long before dawn and, although I made a lengthy ceremonial of getting into my flying togs and packing the effects that I was leaving behind, it still was dark when I left the hotel and drove to the flying-field.

When I arrived at the field, I found that the Cellula had already been trundled out of its hangar into the glare of the powerful beacons, and that Johnson and a dozen mechanics were swarming over the great birdlike flying-boat examining and testing for the hundredth time every minute bolt and wire and screw. 'Well?' I said, as Johnson, oil-can in hand and smeared from head to foot with black grease, came over to where I stood.

He shook his head dubiously. 'Weather don't look right,' he said.

And in fact, almost as he spoke, the lowering clouds dissolved into a fine cold drizzle that blurred the lights and covered my woollen clothing with tiny glistening beads.

We sought refuge under the projecting gable of the hangar, where a dozen or more reporters, officials, and personal friends had already assembled. As the sky paled, the lights were switched off, but there was no sign of the sun and the rain dripped down from the overhanging greyness with dismal persistence.

In my keyed-up state, I was all for making the start, rain

or no rain. Almost any risk or discomfort seemed to me preferable to a postponement of this carefully planned-for and eagerly awaited hour. But after much persuasion, I deferred to the soberer judgement of Johnson and the meteorological experts. An easterly wind offered no promise of clearing, and a special report from Washington confirmed our doubts. Added to this, was the very real immediate danger of attempting to lift our heavily laden craft from the already sodden field. It would have been a childishly foolhardy risk.

By nine o'clock, the rain was beating metallically upon the roof of the hangar and the field was dotted with shallow puddles. The witnesses had long since departed, and Johnson and I stood by dismally, while the mechanics rolled our craft back into the great shed. At length we pulled ourselves away from the field and, returning to the city, went to the Aero Club where we spent most of the day, pretending to occupy ourselves with maps and charts and weather-reports.

The rain streamed on steadily, all day and all night. The next day was no better. On the third there was a brief respite; the rain stopped and our hopes rose. But we looked in vain for a break in the grey vault above us, and by evening a familiar drumming on the window-pane reduced us again to despair.

The days were interminable. We spent several hours each morning in the hangar, pretending to make more perfect our already super-perfect craft. We went over our plans in minutest detail, convincing ourselves that we had overlooked nothing – of which we had already been convinced weeks before! We smoked and read and slept; we played chess and hand-ball and stud-poker, but still each day seemed endless.

On the afternoon of the sixth the wind suddenly shifted, but although we had been prepared for the change by a special report of the Meteorological Bureau, we hailed the event itself with insane joy. We hurried at once to the flying-field and when we arrived there the stiff south-westerly breeze had already swept the grey pall from the sky and a fecund vernal sun was drawing the moisture from the saturated earth.

By the morning of the seventh the field was firmly dry. The breeze had dwindled to a zephyr, and the flaring sun bounded above the horizon into a fleckless sky. Strangely enough, I had slept long and serenely the night before. The long delay had served to dissipate my feverish excitement; it was impossible to maintain oneself at such a pitch for so many days. And so I arrived upon the field feeling fresh and relaxed and giving no more thought to what lay before us than if we had been planning an hour's jaunt over the neighbouring countryside.

In fact, I was even a little late! When I reached the field, some fifty spectators were already gathered about the whirling propeller, and Johnson, in his flying-suit, was posing for a photograph.

'So you decided to come along, did you?' he grinned, as I approached. 'I was just going to leave without you.'

A score of reporters and photographers swarmed about me. I was obliged to pose for innumerable photographs; I was ordered to take off my hat, to smile, to shake hands with Johnson, to smoke a cigarette, to climb into the cockpit and to climb out again. And, once more, the zealous journalists tried to bully or to cajole me into revealing our destination. But upon this point I was adamant; and neither their appeals to my alleged good nature, nor their strictures upon my duty to the public could sway me from my firm resolve not to divulge our objective. They had, of course, been just as unsuccessful with Johnson, and although they all wished us the best of luck, it was obvious that, if we came to grief, they would regard it as the natural and just consequence of our failure to take the press into our confidence.

Perhaps a word or two in explanation of our reticence would not be amiss, if only to make it clear that our silence was not prompted by a mere childish taste for mystification, or by a desire to enhance our own prestige or give our voyage an illusory importance by veiling it in portentous secrecy. On the contrary, it was rather because we wished to minimize our exploit and to prevent it from becoming a matter of planetary – or even trans-spatial – concern that we had decided upon silence.

Consider our position. Although each of us had served with some distinction in his own field – Johnson as a pilot and I as an ethnologist – neither of us could be said to be a figure of world-wide or even of national importance. Yet, here we were, we two relatively obscure men, setting out upon what was perhaps the most hazardous and uncertain voyage in the whole history of discovery and exploration. We were seeking for the first time to establish a human contact with that fascinatingly mysterious land of whose marvels so many alluring rumours had reached us, but of which nothing, literally nothing, was actually known.

It will be seen at once what the effect would have been if we had revealed our purpose. It is almost certain that we should have been asked to make the voyage under the auspices of some learned society, or perhaps even under the auspices of the government. We should have been charged with messages of a formal character to the people and the governmental heads of that far country; perhaps even entrusted with the delicate mission of establishing a diplomatic relationship between our planet and Purilia. And it is certain, too, that once our destination became known the intelligence would somehow or other find its way through the ether and we should arrive in a country prepared for our coming and organized to receive us. In short, the whole voyage would have taken on an official character which would have accorded neither with our temperaments nor with what we hoped to achieve.

It was our wish to visit the country – assuming that the hazardous voyage could be accomplished – in our capacity

8

of private citizens, and, secondarily, as scientists. We wanted to travel quietly and unobtrusively about the country, to mingle unostentatiously with people of every class and every profession, to use our eyes and our ears, and to make observations and notes, unhampered by official duties or public attention. It was obvious that this could be done only if our voyage was unsponsored and unheralded. (Or at least so we believed. We could not guess that, owing to the singular temperaments of the Purilians and the peculiar conditions of Purilian life, we should have been received, no matter what the auspices of our journey, not only without surprise, but with almost complete indifference.)

Furthermore, there was the other danger that official measures might have been taken to prevent our making the voyage at all. Viewed by a matter-of-fact mind, we might have been regarded as merely embarking upon an elaborate and exotic form of suicide. Indeed, in our own less exalted moments, we sometimes took that view of it ourselves. We knew very well that it was as likely as not, perhaps more likely than not, that we should never return. (The fact that poor Johnson did not return had really nothing to do with the probable dangers attendant upon our expedition. It was due merely to one of those grotesque and ironic accidents which persuade one of the folly of all calculation. But I must not anticipate my story!) However, we were independent men without family ties or other obligations and we felt that if we chose to hazard our lives, the choice was ours to make. In short, we did not minimize the risk; we simply decided that it was worth taking. But some well-intentioned friend or meddlesome public official might have taken another view and might, by one means or another, have checked our enterprise at its very outset.

So, all things considered, we had determined upon silence and had contented ourselves with announcing that we were embarking upon a voyage which, if successful, not only would constitute a contribution to science but would prove a matter of general public interest as well. Beyond that, we would disclose nothing, despite the unremitting pressure which was brought to bear upon us. And I might add, in passing, that in the whole voyage itself, and in the lengthy preparations for it, there was no hour more arduous and fatiguing than those which were spent in evading and combating the determined questioning of the well-meaning, the curious, and the officious.

At length the leave-takings came to an end. The last camera-shutter had clicked, the last friendly hand had been wrung, and the last good wish had been uttered. I climbed into the cockpit, where Johnson was already installed, his hand upon one of the dual controls. The little door shut behind me, and I tested the handle to make sure that it was fast.

'All right?' queried Johnson.

'Yes,' I replied.

'Then let's go,' he said.

He pushed the lever noiselessly forward and a brief premonitory quiver ran through the Cellula, as though she really were some great, animate, winged creature, poising herself for a sustained flight. Then, propelled by a hundred helping hands, she glided along the runway, ever so slowly at first, but gathering speed with every yard she traversed. A moment of breathless suspense as she raced toward the field's outer barrier and then a sense of exhilaration as she lifted her great bulk from the ground, slowly but unhesitatingly. We described a great arc and swept in a sharply ascending spiral around the field, high above the flung hats and inaudible shouts of the fifty manikins.

Then we climbed! Straight up, we climbed. The earth fell away from us, single objects became indistinguishable. Towns and fields became mere patches of colour, and then even the colours faded. Sharp contours flattened and dwindled away. Then, beneath our eyes, the earth rounded into its great curves and presently there hung below us a monstrous but rapidly shrinking ball.

We did not speak. We were too exalted for words, too conscious of our splendid and terrible isolation. Now and then, we exchanged an eloquent look, but that was all. Johnson concentrated upon his controls, every sense attuned to the intricate and delicate mechanism which was now our world. It grew colder and I turned my attention to the regulation of the heating coils which kept our cabin at a comfortable, even temperature.

The air grew rarer too and presently we were obliged to don the oxygen masks which Herbert Allen had so carefully and laboriously constructed for us and which were perhaps the most important part of our equipment. We could not have talked now, even had we wished, but, except for this disability and for the slight discomfort of the blood pounding in our temples, we were as much at ease as we should have been in the chart-room of an ocean liner.

It grew constantly darker as we neared the outer limits of the earth's atmosphere. At length, even the last faint glimmer of light faded and, although our chronometer told us that it was only nine in the morning, we found ourselves plunged in utter darkness – the darkness of interstellar space, a darkness inconceivably more profound than the blackest of terrestrial nights.

I cannot hope to convey to the reader the faintest sense of the grandeur of the heavenly pageant that unrolled itself before our bewildered eyes. The profuse stars blazed in whirlpools of green and violet and red. In a great wheel, the constellations of the zodiac marched singing through the heavens. The planets were orbs of liquid fire. Mercury, Venus, Mars, Jupiter – we saw and knew them all; and the distant outer triad, too. But nearest and brightest of all hung a new and strange luminary – unknown to us and yet best-known: the earth!

For many minutes, we surrendered ourselves to the spectacle, and then the serious business of navigation claimed our attention. The second phase of our voyage had begun. With all the terrestrial conditions, we had, of course, been thoroughly familiar and had counted upon a smooth and eventless completion of our passage through the earth's atmosphere. But now we were soaring into the unknown, or at least, the unexperienced. Our calculations, both as to the potentialities of our craft and as to the course of our voyage, had withstood every theoretical test – but, after all, the tests had been only theoretical! It remained to be seen how nearly performance would substantiate theory.

We were heartened and elated by the behaviour of our ship. Our engines sang sweetly and truly and our instruments indicated that speed and fuel consumption were well within the wide margin of error which we had allowed ourselves. The Winsted gravitator, which I had put into operation shortly before we left the earth's atmosphere, was fulfilling the most optimistic predictions of its inventor, and the Cellula rode the ether waves as serenely as a yacht in a sheltered roadstead. Apparently we could rely upon our craft.

It remained now to find our nebulous objective. We did not for an instant doubt the existence of Purilia, nor its location in space, at the approximate position which our charts indicated. But, on the other hand, we did not minimize the possibility of error. Granting the thousand and one inferential proofs of the country's actuality, we could not avoid recognizing the fact that no human had ever set foot or eye upon it. And acknowledging the genius of astronomers, mathematicians, and aerial navigators, we had to admit that even these savants themselves laid no claim to infallibility. And so, when the first minutes of dazzled wonder had passed, we began to take our bearings and to look upon the coruscating suns as merely so many guideposts along our untrodden way.

On the pad that lay between us, I scribbled the suggestion that I relieve Johnson at the controls, so that he could devote his undivided attention to the charts and reckonings. He nodded his assent and I took over the guidance of our swift and pliant chariot. With the aid of an occasional nod or a pencilled word from Johnson, I easily kept the course. Hour succeeded uneventful hour and still we roared blithely through space, for all the world like a pair of suburban motorists on a holiday. Now and then, we passed through a zone of such intense cold that not even our electric coils could withstand it: and once I had to swerve sharply off the course to clear the magnetic field of a great incandescent meteorite. But these were almost welcome reliefs to a singularly monotonous journey.

According to our calculations, we could expect to sight Purilia at about four in the afternoon, and although we both made an ostentatious show of not looking at the chronometer, I for one always knew to the minute exactly what time it was; and I have not the slightest doubt that Johnson did too. Twelve o'clock, one o'clock, two o'clock passed, with wonted regularity, and then, as the hour-hand crept on to three and past it, I became conscious of a quickening of the pulse and a tightening of every muscle and nerve. Johnson bent unremittingly over his charts, but I could see that his swift glances into space were becoming more frequent and that his calculations became more and more prolonged and involved.

Four o'clock passed and half past four. The Cellula roared smoothly and steadily on through the flashing heavens. We exchanged neither look nor comment. For any outward sign of interest or emotion, we might have been commuters on our way to our offices. And indeed there was no occasion for comment. We both knew fully what were the alternatives. We had a six-hour fuel reserve, the absolute maximum that our craft could carry. If we did not sight Purilia by ten o'clock, at the very latest, we had nothing to expect but extinction, and the fact that we did not know what form that extinction would take did not lessen its certainty. Purilia by ten o'clock, or death – there was no other alternative. Actually, however, our margin of safety was less than that, for whereas we had allowed for a retardation of speed or a deviation from our course, the fact was that our actual position in space coincided almost exactly with the theoretical position indicated by our charts. In other words, upon the basis of our position, we knew that we must either sight Purilia soon or else that our calculations were so wrong that we could never hope to reach it. So that the passage of every minute decreased in geometric ratio our chances of attaining our goal.

Five o'clock! Minute followed upon minute. The quarter hour passed and the long pointer crept toward the half-hour. I began, despite any effort, to think back upon the days of my life. I recalled, with sudden vividness, a multitude of opportunities missed, of things that had better been left unsaid or undone, of faces and places – dearer to me than I had known – that I should never see again; and my fancy played rather ruefully with the notion that another ten years would have rounded out gracefully an existence that, at forty, seemed singularly fruitless.

Suddenly, Johnson gripped my arm with such violence that I almost released my hold upon the controls. Startled out of my reverie, I turned and looked at him; his eyes just visible above the oxygen mask were gleaming with excitement and with his extended right arm he pointed into space. I peered into the blackness but saw nothing, except the now familiar and almost hateful stars. Turning back to Johnson's eager look of inquiry, I shook my head negatively. Again he pointed and again I looked in vain. He seized the pencil and scribbled hastily upon the pad. 'Pink cloud,' I read, 'dead ahead.'

Again I stared into space; but for a long time I could see nothing. Then, at length, I discerned, ever so far away, a faint pinkish blur, so indistinct that when I removed my eyes from it for an instant to nod an elated confirmation to Johnson, I had great difficulty in recovering it.

'Purilia?' I queried, on the pad.

'Sure as you're born,' replied Johnson.

The cloud was clearly visible now and growing more distinct every moment. No retrospection now, but only an exultant sense of liberation: a condemned prisoner receiving a reprieve at the foot of the scaffold! But that mood passed quickly too, and I was the man of action again, my brain buzzing with plans and projects.

The cloud spread out densely before us now: a roseate mass of discernible form which filled the heavens and paled the stars. Purilia! Neither of us doubted it for a moment. Our engine churned swiftly on, and my excited fancy seemed to catch a note of exhilaration in its throbbing, as if it, too, were sentient, and, despite its brave performance, had had its own misgivings.

By six o'clock, it was so light that the stars were no longer visible. The earth's orb still shone faintly far below us, but in a few minutes the Cellula plunged boldly into the luminous masses of rosy cloud, and the world of humans and all that pertained to it disappeared from view.

CHAPTER 2

So inured had our eyes become to the black emptiness of celestial night, that we found ourselves blinded and confused by the dense opacity of the mist through which we were now travelling and by the rose-coloured light that permeated it. Actually, we were in greater danger of immediate physical mishap than we had been at any time since we cleared the earth. But there was nothing to do but go boldly ahead and trust to the almost miraculous good fortune which had so far attended us.

Johnson scrawled on the pad. 'See if there's some air,' I read. I nodded, and switching on our Bauerheim bivalvular ventilator, held my ear close to the serrated aperture. After a few moments, I could discern, even above the roaring of our motors, a faint rhythmic pulsation. Unmistakably, the ventilator was pumping air – or, at least, some aeriform gas – into our cabin. With infinite caution, I raised my oxygen mask and inhaled very slowly – not without trepidation, for it was by no means impossible that I might be breathing in some noxious vapour, not only incapable of sustaining human life, but likely to bring my existence to an abrupt end.

As the gas flowed into my lungs, I experienced a choking, gagging sensation; but I resisted the impulse to cough and allowed my chest to fill with the strange effluvium. For a few moments, I panted spasmodically and then slowly my respiratory apparatus adapted itself to the unfamiliar gas; and presently I found myself able to inhale and exhale with something resembling the regularity of normal breathing.

'Whatever it is, you can breathe it,' I shouted into the ear of Johnson, who had been watching me anxiously. He nodded and removed his oxygen mask. For a few moments he gasped and spluttered and then he too began to assimilate the new element. What we were breathing was certainly not the air that pertained to our own planet. It had a quite perceptible density and a curious sweetish taste, which made one experience a slight sensation of nausea. Johnson reported the same symptoms. At first, we attributed our discomfort to the fact that we had eaten nothing since early morning (our oxygen masks had, of course, made eating impossible). We each ate a sandwich now and drank some coffee. But that slight nausea persisted. Indeed, I may say that it persisted throughout my entire sojourn in Purilia; and that, even now, whenever I turn my thoughts to that amazing country, I can taste the strange, sweet flavour of the atmosphere which enshrouds it, and I become conscious of a faint sense of ill-being.

Whether the pinkish mist became thinner, or whether our eyes merely became accustomed to it, I do not know; but in a little while we were able to see much more clearly, and before long we became aware of a solid mass far beneath us which was undoubtedly the land itself.

Indeed, it began presently to take on more and more definite outlines and contours and we were interested and rather surprised to note that, in its larger topographical aspects, Purilia bore a striking resemblance to our own earth. Indeed, had it not been for the slight but persistent discomfort with which we breathed and for the rosy glow with which everything was suffused, we might have believed ourselves to be descending upon the terrestrial scene.

We were still too far aloft to distinguish, with any great clarity, individual objects below us; but suddenly I became aware of two tiny specks, which seemed to be moving in our direction. I called Johnson's attention to them and we regarded them closely. They came nearer and nearer and soon we saw that the moving objects were actually two large biplanes, travelling at terrific speed.

The planes continued to draw rapidly nearer, and when the first was some five hundred yards distant it changed its course and began flying in a great circle. The second plane followed, and it became obvious, from observing the movements of the two, that the second was in frantic pursuit of the first. On and on, the two went, the pursuer drawing closer and closer to its quarry. Then, all at once, I was amazed to see what appeared to be a living object making its way, perilously, along the wing of the first plane.

'Look,' shouted Johnson, 'it's a girl!'

And indeed it was! A slender female figure was actually walking along the wing of the speeding plane. Then, as we strained our startled eyes, we observed a most incredible phenomenon. The figure of the girl, which, as I have said, was a quarter-mile or more away, suddenly swelled to such gigantic proportions that it seemed to be almost within reach of our hands. Indeed, so alarming was the figure's proximity, that Johnson made the Cellula swerve sharply away. As for me, I was so filled with amazement that I barely had time to note that the girl was young and beautiful and apparently in deep distress (as indeed she might well have been in her precarious situation).

The gigantic apparition vanished as quickly as it had come, and now we saw the distant planes again, the second drawing ever closer and closer to the first. But we observed now that there was a second figure upon the wing of the pursued plane: the figure of a man advancing with slow deliberation toward the girl, who now stood perched almost upon the tip of the wing.

We had no time, however, to marvel at this spectacle, for again a huge apparition hurled itself at the very window of our cabin. Only this time, it was the face of the man that thrust itself into our faces, and, startled though we were, we could not fail to take cognizance of the lecherous look which it wore. Never before had I seen a face so disfigured by unbridled lust!

'Looks as if he's trying to make her,' shouted Johnson (with his habitual colloquial bluntness of speech), as the hateful visage disappeared and we saw its distant owner creeping slowly along the wing of the plane, toward the terrified girl. It was truly a horrible situation and both the girl's profound agitation and her rash behaviour were readily understandable now.

Still nearer drew the man. He was almost touching her now and she was recoiling from him with a horror which was fully revealed to us by another of those amazing optical phenomena which brought her distressed features within six inches of our eyes.

We were filled with pity and with terror; and with a sense of our own helplessness to render aid. Then, as that distraught face vanished, we were astonished and relieved to see that the second plane was circling directly above the first and that a man was lowering a rope-ladder within easy reach of the girl. For an instant, the man's looming face revealed him as young and handsome, and then as the planes came into view again, we saw, to our delight, that the girl was climbing up the rope-ladder out of the clutches of her pursuer.

But the next instant our delight changed to horror, for the libertine drew a revolver and, firing at the rope-ladder, just above the hand of the ascending girl, severed the strands of one of the latter's vertical supports so that she hung there swinging perilously in mid-air, suspended only by a single rope, from the fuselage of the rapidly moving plane. Fortunately, the young man above was equal to the occasion. Leaning far over the edge of the wing, he circled the waist of the terrified girl with his right arm and drew her firmly up to the comparative safety of the wing's surface.

I say comparative safety, because it soon became obvious that the danger was by no means over. As the second plane drew away from the first, the baulked scoundrel below clutched at the dangling rope and clambered deftly up beside the young man and the girl. The girl retreated along the wing of the plane, while the two men grappled fiercely. They clawed and pummelled each other savagely, apparently heedless of their precarious situation. As for the girl, it scarcely needed the acreage of her distressed visage to make us conscious of her emotional disturbance.

Then we gasped with dismay, as the older man succeeded in pushing the younger over the edge of the wing. It seemed as though it were all over with him indeed. But, with astounding presence of mind, the youth grasped one of the ailerons and hung there: suspended over space by one hand! The other man now drew a large knife from his pocket and leaned over the edge of the wing. His intention was unmistakable: he was going to sever the fingers by which the young man clung to life. I tried to avert my eyes but could not – and then, just as the hand clutching the knife approached the young man's fingers, the plane suddenly lurched and the scoundrel was hurtled into space!

'Serves him damn good and right!' shouted Johnson

excitedly, into my ear. I nodded assent, and turning my eyes toward the distant planes again, I saw that the young man had climbed up on the wing, where the girl was eagerly awaiting him. It was obvious that they were lovers. And indeed, he took her tenderly in his arms and, as their lips met, their united faces hurled themselves upon us. Then we saw them no more. The two planes had disappeared also, and we were surprised to find that our absorption in the events that I have described had made us unmindful of the fact that we had descended sufficiently to make out the details of the Purilian landscape.

We had no time now to comment upon the recent startling occurrences nor even to seek an explanation for those singular optical illusions which astonished us more than anything else that had happened. Although I shall have occasion more than once in this work to speak of these sudden apparitions – which, by the way, never failed to fill me with amazement and consternation – I may as well confess, at the outset, that I have never found a satisfactory explanation for them. Of the hundreds of Purilians whom I plied with questions, not one was able to offer me any enlightenment upon this subject. In fact, I never succeeded in making anyone understand the nature of my inquiry, for these phenomena are so much an integral part of the Purilian world that they are accepted as unconsciously as we humans accept the functioning of the glands or the circulation of the blood. And whereas the scientists among us make these latter the subjects of scientific investigation, Purilia, as I shall have occasion to explain later, is poor in scientists – research and the pursuit of pure knowledge being, indeed, almost unknown there. So that what we learned of the peculiarities of the country was gleaned almost entirely from our own observations and deductions. And the only explanation I can offer for the aberrations of which I speak, is that I attribute them to some special property of the atmosphere, entirely foreign to our planet and peculiar to

Purilia. But this is, frankly, nothing more than an hypothesis.

The panorama that spread out below us bore a striking similarity to the physiognomy of our own world. There were rivers and lakes, fields and hills, cities and towns. As we had still a considerable fuel reserve, we decided to fly over the countryside while it was yet light, in order to obtain a wide view before descending for a more detailed investigation.

For some time now, I had noticed a curious vibration which seemed to have nothing to do with our craft, but appeared rather to be occasioned by something outside it. Johnson noticed it too and we tried to find some explanation for it. We seemed lapped in an all-enveloping wave-like pulsation. The Cellula was continuing to perform perfectly and since the vibration, whatever its cause, did not seem to impede our progress, we determined to think no more of it until such time as we could ascertain its source.

For an hour or more, we circled over the country. The scene was pleasing to the eye. There were many fine large estates, surrounding magnificent houses of palatial dimensions. And there were many vine-clad cottages too, the homes, no doubt, of the humbler folk. Then there were great cities with piled towers, their streets teeming with vehicles and people. There seemed, also, to be vast tracts of desert and of grazing land, and we flew over several mountain-ranges, cleft with deep cañons. I was surprised to note that there was no apparent evidence of industrial activity. The great number of automobiles, railway-systems, steamships, and aeroplanes which were visible everywhere, clearly evidenced a mechanical civilization, but I looked in vain for factory chimneys, blast furnaces, slag heaps, or any of the other familiar concomitants of an industrialized world.

One feature of the landscape, which we viewed with great satisfaction, was the profusion of church-spires, in both city and country. It was indeed a most reassuring omen, for it betokened that the Purilians were a civilized and a godly people and that we had little to fear on the score of personal safety. The aerial encounter which we had just witnessed should have prepared us, no doubt, to find the country less peaceable than its serene and smiling aspect made it appear; but naturally we had looked upon that dramatic interlude as a most unusual occurrence. We had yet to learn that one could not travel a hundred miles nor live a day in Purilia without seeing a dozen such happenings!

As evening approached, we began to look about for a landing place. We had agreed that we should make our descent in some rural district, rather than in the vicinity of a town or city where not only might our arrival make us objects of popular curiosity, but we should be subjected at once to so many complex and varied stimuli that we should have difficulty in making accurate observations. From what we had seen of the three Purilians in mid-air, we surmised that the people of the country bore a great resemblance both in appearance and in dress to the inhabitants of the earth. And we hoped that, if we could make our landing unobserved, we might succeed, for a time at least, in concealing the fact that we were humans. In any case, we were sure that our arrival would create much less stir in the country than in some densely populated area

Accordingly, we selected a large level meadow in the vicinity of some scattered farmhouses and after circling low over the field, in order to ascertain the nature of the terrain, we glided down and brought the Cellula gently to rest upon the soil of Purilia – our amazing journey at an end, and our mysterious goal attained.

22

CHAPTER 3

JOHNSON switched off the ignition and, as the roaring of our engines ceased abruptly, I became even more conscious of the curious vibrations which I had felt ever since we had entered the Purilian atmosphere. But I could see nothing which might account for them, and, as I was temporarily deafened (as one usually is after a flight of such duration), I could hear nothing, either. Indeed, for a time, we had to shout at each other in order to make ourselves understood.

With alacrity, we struggled out of our confined seats. It was a warm spring evening and we felt uncomfortably hot. We helped each other out of our heavy outer garments and painfully stretched our stiffened limbs. We had worn our flying suits over our ordinary street clothes, and had no baggage other than a small valise, containing a change of linen and a few toilet necessities; every permissible ounce had gone to fuel and mechanical equipment.

I opened the door of the cockpit and we stepped, or rather staggered, out upon the ground. Freed from our cramped quarters, and the tension of nerves and muscles relaxed, we revived quickly. Our bodies became flexible again, our eyes no longer strained into space, and our normal hearing was restored.

'Music!' exclaimed Johnson and I, at the same instant. For with the recovery of our hearing, we became aware that the air was filled with harmonious sound. Flooded, I might better have said, for great waves of mellow harmony rolled about us and over us, filling heaven and earth (if I may apply these worldly terms to the Purilian atmosphere and soil) with incessant pulsation. Undoubtedly, this was the cause of the strange vibrations. The music was all-enveloping, all-encompassing; it could almost be touched, almost seen, so inescapable and overpowering were its cadences.

We looked about for the source of these great billows of sound. But we could not discover it; nor indeed, during our entire visit to Purilia, did we ever succeed in discovering it. The people, as I have already said, are not given to scientific inquiry and they accept the ever-present harmony with the same unquestioning indifference with which they accept all the physical conditions of their unique world.

It is difficult to convey to the terrestrial reader, to whom music is an accidental and occasional phenomenon, the effect of living and moving in a world in which melody is as much a condition of life as are light and air. But let the reader try to fancy himself lapped every moment of his existence, waking or sleeping, in liquid, swooning sound, for ever rising and falling, falling and rising, and wrapping itself about him like a caressing garment. The effect is indescribable. It is like the semi-stupor of an habitual intoxication: an inebriety without intervals of either sobriety or complete unconsciousness. It is insidious and irresistible; the hardest head and the stoutest organism cannot withstand it. And I dare say that more than once in this record of Purilia, the sensitive reader will catch echoes and overtones of that omnipresent harmony; now pathetic, now gay, now ominous, now martial, now tender, but always awakening familiar memories, always swellingly mellifluous, and always surcharged with a slight but unmistakable tremolo.

While we were still puzzling over the origin of the strange music, we were not a little surprised to hear a voice say: 'Spring comes early to the Purilian hills.'

We looked about for the speaker, but in vain. Although it was still light enough to see clearly, there was no one visible. And indeed the voice, while quite audible even above the pervasive music, did not appear to come from anyone near at hand; it seemed rather, like the music itself, to emanate from some all-permeating but indeterminable source. It was a round, suave, unctuous voice, lilting and cadenced, and curiously impersonal. And although the tone in which it made its interesting observation about spring was one of helpful courtesy, there was in it, too, a note of authoritative firmness.

But these reflections came later. For, scarcely had the voice ceased, when a robin's nest on the branch of a tree near by (which we had not hithertofore noticed), suddenly swelled to such enormous proportions, that we involuntarily stepped back in alarm. The bird, which was industriously feeding its hungry young, with loving maternal solicitude, appeared for an instant to be as large as some fabulous roc. Then it shrank as suddenly as it had swelled and we saw that it was a mere robin after all. But with the deflation of the robin, a distant lamb, tottering across the field, loomed elephantine. And as it, in turn, receded, a modest crocus, just raising its head in the tender grass, expanded and shot upwards with tropical luxuriance.

'What's the idea anyhow?' asked Johnson a little resentfully. (And it must be confessed that, until one grew to expect them as a matter of course, these gigantic apparitions were not a little disconcerting.)

'I don't know, I'm sure,' I replied. 'But you'll notice,' I added, 'that they all seem to bear out the pronouncement about spring.'

No other explanation presented itself to us, and we waited, with enforced patience, while a romping colt, a rippling brook, and a curly-headed child in a pinafore, fondling a new-born kitten – all swollen to heroic stature – impinged themselves upon us.

The procession of monstrosities concluded, we started across the fields in the direction of a farmhouse which we had seen from the air. Night was approaching and it was expedient to seek shelter. We had taken only a few steps, however, when Johnson hastily seized my arm and cried, 'Look!' I looked in the direction which he indicated, and, from behind a tree near by, I saw the head of a young and beautiful girl, who peered at us coyly.

'Why.' I exclaimed in amazement, 'it's the girl we saw up there on the wing of that plane!'

Before Johnson could reply, the strange disembodied voice that we had already heard, spoke again. 'For nineteen summers.' it said in its curiously impersonal accents, 'Pansy Malone grew among the verdant fields of Purilia, a lovely unspoiled child of Nature.'

The voice ceased and the face, to whose owner this conveniently informative announcement undoubtedly referred, rushed forward at us expansively, and then receded again. Then the girl, herself, stepped from behind the tree and came toward us.

She was – as the voice had indicated – indeed a lovely creature. And a first glance seemed to confirm the suggestion that she was native to the countryside: the daughter of a humble farmer perhaps. Barefoot and dressed in well-fitting rags, she leaned daintily upon the handle of a rake (which, upon reflection, struck me as a little odd, for it was scarcely the season for haying).

A closer scrutiny, however, raised many puzzling doubts as to the accuracy of the descriptive announcement. By terrestrial standards, I should have thought her to be thirty rather than nineteen, and her person seemed to belie a life of arduous toil and exposure to the elements. Although she was hatless, her skin was snowy and unblemished. Her lips were small bows of unusual perfection and each eyelash stiffly proclaimed its individual existence. Her hair, which was literally a mass of golden ringlets, might well have been proclaimed a triumph of tonsorial art. The hand which clasped the rake (as well as the other hand, which fingered the hem of her charmingly tattered dress) was soft and white, and the finger-nails were well-shaped and beautifully polished and tinted. And I was not a little surprised to observe that the dainty toes, that nestled modestly in the grass, were handsomely manicured, too. But I remembered that I was in a strange country and I surmised that the conditions of rural life in Purilia are unlike our own (which I subsequently discovered to be the case).

'Good evening,' I said to the lovely creature. 'We're strangers here and are looking for a place to spend the night.'

'I live with my widowed mother in a simple cottage,' replied Miss Malone, her face swelling, 'but such as it is, you're welcome to share it.'

We were naturally a little hesitant about accepting this magnanimous offer; but the girl seemed so genuine in her generous simplicity that we readily overcame our scruples. And I must add that the prospect of being under the same roof with this beautiful maiden did not diminish my willingness to accept. I was convinced by now that I was mistaken in my first impression: she was not the girl whose perilous aerial adventure we had witnessed. But there was, between the two, more than one point of striking resemblance, and I wondered whether there could be by any chance a kinship between them, or whether the characteristics I noted in both were common to all Purilian young womankind. (The latter conjecture was, of course, correct; and I shall have occasion in the course of this narrative to speak at length of the curious caste-system which is one of the most remarkable institutions of Purilia.)

Pansy (as we soon learned to call her) assured us that the Cellula could be safely left in the field where we had brought it to rest. She seemed to take our sudden arrival, out of space, quite as a matter of course and showed no curiosity concerning either ourselves or our journey. I did not know whether to attribute this singular lack of interest to maidenly reserve or to the tact of a considerate hostess, who refrains from plying her guests with embarrassing questions. Had I been a little more experienced in the ways of the country, I should have known that events which, to us, would appear incredibly extraordinary are matters of such every-day occurrence in Purilia, that they are scarcely noticed, much less questioned. (On the other hand, I have seen the soberest and most mature Purilians thrown into a state of almost unbelievable consternation by what seemed to me the most trivial incident -- the arrival of a letter, for example, or the ringing of a door-bell.)

We took our few personal effects and followed Pansy across the fields. It developed that the cottage in which she lived was the very one which we had observed and at which we had intended to ask shelter. It was twilight now and, as I looked toward the distant hills, I saw a herd of cows making their way slowly in single file along the very ridges, their bodies sharply silhouetted against the sky.

Again the voice of that incorporeal presence was heard. 'The lovely hour of twilight,' it said, 'when the sun sinks behind the western hills and man and beast return homeward after the day's toil.'

It was obvious, by now, that these observations called for neither reply nor comment, but were merely encyclopaedic in character, supplying the listener with much valuable information, charged with more than a dash of gentle philosophy to sweeten it.

As we approached the house, there was still enough light to enable us to discern clearly its essential characteristics. It was a neat little white cottage, with a sloping roof, and dainty curtains at the windows. In front, was a charming little flower-garden and the cottage itself was covered with clambering rose-vines. I was pleased to note that, although it was still early in May, the roses were in full bloom and the air was filled with their fragrance.

'Pretty nice little place you got here,' said Johnson, as we entered the little gate and walked up the neatly gravelled path to the cottage.

Pansy stopped, her hand upon the latch, and turned toward us. Her face distended, until it blotted out the cottage itself.

'It's the most beautiful house in the world,' she said, with simple feeling. 'It's home.'

Then her face shrank to its normal dimensions once more. And lifting the latch, she opened the door of the cottage and we all entered.

CHAPTER 4

PANSY conducted us to the sitting-room of the cottage: a small room, modestly furnished, but proclaiming by its immaculate cleanliness the gentility of its inhabitants. At a table, beside a lighted oil-lamp, sat an aged woman, who I supposed was Pansy's mother. And as though to confirm this surmise, the Presence (for so I had come to term the disembodied voice that accompanied us) announced dispassionately: 'Mrs Malone, Pansy's mother, old before her time with work and worry.'

I was grateful for this explanation of Mrs Malone's apparent age. To the uninstructed eye, she seemed seventy, at the very least, and, since we knew that Pansy was only nineteen, the discrepancy would else have been a puzzling one. Mrs Malone did not observe our entrance and so we had ample opportunity to scrutinize her. She was a sweet-faced gentlewoman, with soft white hair, parted severely in the middle. The sombreness of her simple black dress (indicative no doubt of her widowhood) was relieved by a collar of hand-made lace of delicate workmanship, and although the evening was a mild one she wore a woollen shawl about her stooped shoulders.

When we entered, she was wholly absorbed in the contemplation of a framed photograph, which she held in her hand. Suddenly, this photograph filled the room and we saw that it represented a young and handsome man. 'Hoping against hope,' observed the Presence, 'for news of her only son, absent from home for two weary years.'

Mrs Malone sighed deeply and shook her head sorrowfully;

and then, two great tears trickled slowly down her furrowed cheeks. It was indeed an affecting spectacle, and as I glanced at Pansy I saw that two globular tears, of a size that did credit to her sensibilities, were proceeding slowly down her lovely cheeks, too. I must confess that my own eyes were not free from moisture; and, as for Johnson, he blew his nose with such vigour that Mrs Malone could no longer fail to be aware of our presence.

Hastily, she returned the photograph to its accustomed place, upon the table, and, smiling through her tears, rose to greet us. She nodded slowly, as Pansy explained our presence, and then she said, in a sweet quavering voice: 'Strangers are always welcome here; and I hope my boy has found a welcome under some mother's roof, too.'

We could see that her tragedy was uppermost in her thoughts, and in fact, when Pansy left the room to make preparations for the evening meal, the elderly woman proceeded, at once, to acquaint us with the details of her son's disappearance. It seems that the lad – Charlie by name – had had occasion to visit a neighbouring town, in connexion with some business relating to the farm, the nature of which I could not clearly understand. (There is, I discovered later, a curious vagueness and uncertainty about all such details of Purilian life. The Purilians are essentially an emotional people, with a marked lack of interest in the practical minutiae of daily existence.) At any rate, the boy, during his visit to the town, fell in with some evil companions and, despite his sterling character and habitual sobriety, allowed these scoundrels to ply him with drink and to lure him to some low gambling den.

A drunken brawl ensued, in the course of which Charlie was rendered unconscious by a blow upon the head – the unhappy victim of foul play! His sodden companions fled in craven terror, leaving him for dead. But when one of them, more humane than the rest, returned to the scene of the mêlée, Charlie had disappeared! No trace of him had ever been found; and, although two years had elapsed, the fond mother still waited, each day, some confirmation of her maternal conviction that the boy was alive and well.

It was a pitiable tale and, although I strove to cheer the unhappy woman, I could not but feel that her hopes were groundless. But had I not been a new arrival in the country I should have thought otherwise; for I had not been many days in Purilia, ere I learned that such disappearances are the rule, rather than the exception, and that the missing person always turns up, safe and sound, and not a whit the worse for the frightful experiences, which he invariably undergoes during his absence (and this, as the reader will learn, proved to be the case with Charlie). In fact, I doubt if there is a family in all of rural Purilia whose annals do not contain the record of, not one, but many such misadventures. But this happy land is presided over by a sort of poetic justice which so orders matters that intense suffering is always succeeded by a more than compensating happiness. And more than once during my sojourn in Purilia, I had occasion to wish that our planet could know a measure of such harmony!

While we were still commiserating the unhappy mother, Pansy appeared, clad in even more fetching tatters than before, and announced supper. We adjourned to the dining-room and, as we seated ourselves at the table, upon which several dishes of steaming viands were already displayed, a burly, jovial-faced fellow, in overalls, entered hurriedly from the kitchen. As he approached the table he stumbled awkwardly over a rug and lurched against the sideboard, dislodging a plate, which fell upon his head and broke into a dozen fragments. I was alarmed for his safety, but was reassured, when I observed that both Pansy and her mother were smiling indulgently, and that the fellow himself, although he rubbed his head ruefully, seemed none the worse for the mishap. Indeed, he took his place briskly at the table; and as he tied an enormous napkin under his chin the

Presence obligingly remarked: 'Jim Slocum, the hired man, never ate peas for fear of cutting his mouth.'

I had no time to reflect upon this rather cryptic utterance, for my attention was immediately engaged by Jim's remarkable behaviour. Although no one had yet been served, he leaned far across the table, toward the dishes of food, and heaped his own plate mountain-high. Then, bending close over the plate, he began consuming the food, with the most alarming rapidity, plying both knife and fork vigorously, his eyes bulging and his cheeks distended. It was far from a pleasant spectacle and I rather expected that Pansy or her mother would rebuke the man. But this, their good nature would not allow, and they contented themselves with little smiles and head-shakings, in which faint deprecation and tolerant amusement were mingled.

What remained of the food was divided among the rest of us. Johnson and I were tolerably hungry and ate with enjoyment; but Pansy picked at her food, with an apparent lack of appetite, which I thought surprising in a healthy country girl; as for Mrs Malone, she ate almost nothing. The mother's abstinence, I attributed correctly to her abiding grief; but it was not until I had been some time in Purilia that I learned that a hearty appetite in Pansy would have been regarded as a reprehensible evidence of carnality, and unbecoming to a young and modest girl. For these beautiful creatures, as I shall have occasion to explain, form a high and noble caste and are consecrated to a life of emotional ecstasy and spiritual suffering into which fleshly concerns do not enter.

Soon after the beginning of the meal, an untoward incident occurred. It seems that Jim, the hired man, had sprinkled his food liberally with the contents of the pepper-shaker, under the mistaken impression that it was the salt. The consequence was disastrous, for, no sooner had he conveyed an enormous forkful of the peppery food to his mouth than such a coughing and spluttering ensued as I had never before witnessed. In his distress, the fellow threshed about

32

frantically with the result that he spilled a cup of scalding coffee into his lap. This, naturally, caused him to roar with pain and to leap up from his chair, upsetting it as he did so. Then he rushed toward the kitchen, upsetting another chair, and tripping over the door-sill, which caused him to plunge head-first into a pail of whitewash, which happened to be standing just inside the kitchen door. He emerged from the pail, gasping and coughing, his entire head and face covered with whitewash – a most lamentable spectacle! To make matters worse, as he struggled to his feet, he slipped upon a cake of soap, which happened to be lying on the kitchen floor, and slid out of sight, with a great crash and a clatter of pots and pans, which apparently he dislodged in his fall. Johnson and I were disposed to rush to his assistance, but the quiet, indulgent smiles of Pansy and her mother made us understand that all this was a matter of ordinary occurrence and that there was no occasion whatever for alarm.

But suddenly their smiles vanished, and now they did exhibit alarm – and grave alarm, indeed! The apparent cause of this transformation was nothing more consequential than a knock upon the door, although from the degree of agitation which they both displayed I should have surmised some major catastrophe. They stared at each other, in undisguised terror, and then, as the knock was repeated, Pansy walked, or rather tottered, to the door and opened it.

A man entered the room, and, as he came forward into the light, Johnson whispered excitedly to me: 'Say, ain't that the bird that we saw taking a nose dive off that plane up there?' And certainly the man bore a striking resemblance to the unspeakable scoundrel whom we had seen receive his just deserts, in that dramatic interlude which heralded our arrival in Purilia. It was not he, of course; but our unfamiliarity with the Purilian caste-marks made our mistake a natural one.

I assumed that the Presence would apprise us of the man's identity, and I was not disappointed, for almost instantly, the voice observed blandly: 'Horace Millwood, not content with his ill-gotten millions, had set his heart upon a fairer treasure.' I scrutinized Millwood sharply and I must confess that I did not like his looks. He was handsome enough, as he stood there in his fashionable riding clothes – a riding-crop in his hands and two great hounds snarling at his heels – but there was something in his eye that bespoke libidinous desire, and my heart misgave me with the sudden fear that Pansy was the treasure he desired, and that he boded her no good. One more conversant with the peculiarities of Purilia would have detected two infallible evidences of the man's knavery: the growth of hair upon his upper lip, and his failure to remove his hat in the presence of the two gentle-women.

Millwood cast a sneering, supercilious glance about the room and then, with a threatening gesture of his riding-crop, bade the dogs be quiet. The animals fawned silently at his feet, as though they knew only too well the consequences of disobedience. Pansy and her mother, their hands clutching their bosoms, waited for him to speak.

'I have come for the rent,' said Millwood. 'I suppose you know that it's two weeks overdue.'

I understood, at once, that Millwood was the Malones' landlord; but I was more than a little surprised that this millionaire should take the trouble to call in person to collect the rent of so humble a cottage. I suspected some ulterior motive and events proved that I was not wrong.

Pansy's face mirrored her distress. 'Just give us a few days more,' she pleaded. 'I'm expecting a letter, from my uncle, with the money in it.'

'I've heard that story before,' sneered Millwood. His callousness made my blood boil and, as for Johnson, he would have struck the fellow had I not restrained him. But I should have withheld my restraining hand had I known that, at that very moment, the letter in question lay in Mill-wood's pocket, filched from the mails by the local postmaster,

34

who was one of Millwood's tools. (The Purilian post-office is notorious for its inefficiency and corruptness. Again and again I heard of letters of the utmost importance being either stolen or misdelivered, always with the most dire consequences.)

Mrs Malone now sought to soften Millwood. 'You would not have the heart to turn us out of our home,' she said.

But Millwood was adamant. 'I can wait no longer,' he replied. 'You must pay the rent to-morrow, or get out of the house.' And then turning to Pansy he added significantly, 'Unless, of course, you have changed your mind.'

Pansy looked at him unflinchingly. 'I cannot marry you, Mr Millwood,' she said with quiet dignity. 'I do not love you.'

A scowl distorted Millwood's enlarged features. 'Very well,' he said, with an angry sneer, 'then there's nothing more to be said' – and, turning abruptly, he stalked out of the room, followed by the two savage dogs.

When he had left, Pansy did not attempt to conceal her distress. She gave full vent to her grief; and her mother's attempts to comfort her were in vain. It was clear to me now that Millwood was using the Malones' pecuniary difficulties as means to force the unwilling Pansy into a marriage with him. We discussed the situation at length with the two wretched women; but it seemed quite hopeless, for Pansy, it developed, had fallen victim to the Purilian land-tenure system, which is one of the country's most flagrant evils. And here the reader will no doubt require a word of explanation.

In Purilia, practically all the small rural homesteads are controlled by a class of unscrupulous wealthy men who, either as landlords or mortgagees, rule the economic destinies of the humble homesteaders. The agriculture of the country is upon a most unsound economic basis, and the rural population is engaged in a constant struggle to meet rent and interest payments which, under this most inequitable system, are perpetually due. To aggravate matters, these grasping landowners are always irresistibly attracted to the fair young daughters of their unfortunate tenants and, by ill-chance, this attraction is never reciprocal. So that there is scarcely a Purilian maiden, of rural origin, who is not, at one time or another in her life, faced with the devastating alternatives of allowing her aged parents to be turned out of doors, or of giving herself in marriage (or in many cases, I regret to say, to a state far less honourable than marriage) to one of these agrarian despots. It is a flagrant and a shameful condition and I marvel that nothing is done about it. Fortunately, in every such case that came to my attention (and their number is incalculable), the imperilled maiden managed, by some means or other, to escape her dilemma and to bring the affair to a happy conclusion.

But, at the moment of Millwood's departure, things looked black indeed for the Malones; and, after seeking in vain for some solution, we mounted the stairs with heavy hearts, to retire for the night.

I had been assigned to the small bedroom which had formerly housed the absent Charlie, and I recognized this courtesy as a token of the esteem in which the Malones already held me; for they regarded the room as a sort of shrine and would never have allowed its threshold to be crossed by one in whom they did not repose a great degree of confidence.

As I was about to retire, I chanced to look out of the little window. A full moon had risen and, along the very ridge of the distant hills, a herd of deer were proceeding slowly in single file, their bodies silhouetted sharply against the sky. It was a lovely sight, and, for some unaccountable reason, I interpreted it as symbol of hope and a sign of better things to follow. I went to bed, with a lightened heart, confident that Pansy, standing at *her* little window, had seen the cheering spectacle too, and had found comfort in it.

CHAPTER 5

NEXT morning, before breakfast, Johnson and I debated upon our next step. Naturally, we were eager to continue our exploration of the country; but, at the same time, we did not feel justified in deserting the Malones in their distress, especially in view of the kindness with which they had received us. We had scarcely expected, of course, to become involved in the private affairs of the Purilians; but the exigencies of the situation demanded that we make some attempt to assist the unfortunate women. (Furthermore, as the reader has perhaps already surmised, Pansy had awakened in me an interest which could not be wholly ascribed to the compassion evoked by her misfortunes, and I was glad enough for so colourable an excuse for remaining near her.) Accordingly, we agreed that the least we could do would be to offer to defer our departure long enough to enable us to attempt some assistance to the Malones in their difficulties.

The two ladies accepted our offer, with a gratitude that was almost effusive. The sight of Pansy's brimming eyes and sweet, sad smile was in itself a sufficient compensation for the alteration in our plans; and I was deeply touched, too, when Mrs Malone placed a wrinkled hand upon each of my shoulders, and said, in a voice quivering with emotion: 'Accept a mother's blessing, sir.'

Our decision taken, we turned our attention to making some temporary disposition of the Cellula. We learned from Pansy that there was a large empty barn upon the farm, which would serve as a hangar. Immediately after breakfast, Pansy conducted us to the field where we had left the plane; and, in a short time, the Cellula was safely housed in the barn.

On the way back to the cottage, we chanced to pass a spring which bubbled out, between two large rocks, into a little pool. Johnson stooped to drink from the pool, and then, suddenly, drew back in amazement. 'Look!' he exclaimed excitedly, pointing to the pool. I bent down beside him and to my amazement saw that the surface of the pool was covered with an iridescent scum.

'Oil!' I cried; and Johnson nodded his excited confirmation. There could be no doubt about it. The land was obviously rich in oil deposits – beneath the worthless expanse of meadowland lay a reservoir of liquid wealth. We explained the situation to Pansy and, for a long, long time, I feasted my eyes upon her amplified features, where slowly dawning comprehension was succeeded by ecstatic joy.

But our jubilation was short-lived. Suddenly, Johnson's sharp eyes detected, not five feet from the pool, the distinct imprint of a pair of riding-boots, and beside it, a riding-crop, which we recognized instantly as Millwood's. It seemed clear now that Millwood had been there before us: the riding-crop, which he must have dropped accidentally, gave him away. And a moment later Johnson, stooping again, picked up a piece of paper which he read hastily and handed to us with an angry ejaculation.

The paper proved to be a letter addressed to Millwood, which he must have dropped accidentally. In the circumstances, I felt quite justified in reading it. It was a communication from the president of an oil syndicate offering Millwood a million dollars for the Malone farm. As I read the letter to Pansy, I was distressed to see her joy give way to despair. And when I had finished, she explained in indignant accents the depths of Millwood's depravity. Not only was he trying to coerce Pansy into a distasteful marriage, but he was scheming to rob the Malones of the fortune that lay almost within their grasp.

I was a little puzzled by this, for it seemed to me that, if Millwood actually did turn the women out of their home, he could not hope to win Pansy's hand; and I wondered too if

Millwood, as the actual owner of the land, did not have a claim upon its mineral deposits. But Pansy's distress was so acute that I forbore to harass her with perplexing questions and chose to attribute these seeming inconsistencies to my own ignorance of the ways of the country.

Johnson, always a man of action, was all for confronting Millwood, at once, and forcing the issue. But I, being of a more passive temperament, counselled less violent measures and suggested taking legal advice. Unfortunately, my counsel prevailed. Could I have foreseen the almost incredible consequences of what I regarded merely as a piece of judicious advice, I firmly believe that I should have hurried into the cockpit of the Cellula with Johnson and flown back to the earth forthwith!

Pansy informed us that there was a lawyer in the town near by, and we decided to visit him at once. We returned to the cottage and arranged with Jim, the hired man, who was the possessor of a rather decrepit automobile, to drive us into the town.

A half-hour later, we took our departure. Pansy had changed her dress again and besides had donned her shoes and stockings and a very charming hat, which set off her golden curls and flowerlike face to great advantage. She was truly a lovely creature, and if I say that my heart fluttered, the reader will not have far to seek for the reason.

Jim arrayed himself, for the visit to town, in the most remarkable raiment I had ever seen. He wore a suit of large black-and-white checks, a red necktie, in which glistened an enormous paste horseshoe, patent-leather shoes with cloth tops and a pearl-grey derby, which came down over his ears. In his buttonhole was a sunflower and he carried a bamboo cane. He was a comical spectacle, indeed, and even Pansy, in all her agitation, could not refrain from smiling.

We entered the car, which Jim finally succeeded in starting – although not without first being knocked down several times, in his efforts to turn the crank. Then we drove off and, as I looked back, I saw the receding figure of Mrs Malone, standing wistfully at the gate of the little rose-covered cottage.

Although the town was only a few miles distant, the journey was one of the most hazardous I had ever undertaken. No one who has not travelled along a Purilian road or street can conceive of the perils of such a journey. The whole country is in the most alarming state of lawlessness, and the public highways are infested with fugitives from justice and their pursuers; with young and beautiful girls fleeing from their would-be abductors; with handsome young men trying to out-distance dark-skinned bandits; with lowly persons closely pursued by ferocious wild animals; with armed troops hastening to the relief of imperilled garrisons; and with frantic messengers spreading the news of impending disasters. So that it is almost impossible to set foot out of doors without danger of colliding with some person who is running at a breakneck pace; or of actual annihilation beneath stampeding hoofs or the wheels of vehicles proceeding with reckless speed.

Several times on our way to the town, our lives were endangered by careering automobiles which wove a darting zigzag course through the traffic, and missed colliding with us by bare inches. To make matters worse, shots were frequently exchanged between the occupants of the pursued and the pursuing cars. Once I saw a car go plunging headlong over a steep embankment. Again I saw a rustic, on an ancient bicycle, overtaken by a bull which was pursuing him. The bull tossed the unfortunate fellow high into the air and, when last I saw him, he was hanging precariously from the branch of a tree by the seat of his trousers, with the bull pawing the ground beneath.

And, once, a rather more ludicrous incident interrupted our journey. When we were about half-way to the town, the engine of our car suddenly ceased to function, and Jim descended to crank it again. While he was bending over the crank, a car going at an incredible rate of speed passed close by him and, as there happened to be a large puddle in the road just at that point, splashed the poor fellow from head to foot. As he arose, we saw that he was entirely covered with thick, black mud, which had, of course, completely ruined his showy finery. He shook his fist violently at the already distant car, and then, spluttering mud as he went, started down the road in obviously futile pursuit. We could not help laughing at his sorry plight.

Johnson took Jim's place as chauffeur, and we proceeded to the town. Pansy explained that the traffic was unusually dense that day, because of the fact that an itinerant circus was giving some performances in a large field just outside the town. Johnson, who had an insatiable appetite for all such exhibitions, was greatly interested and expressed the hope that we should have an opportunity to visit the circus. I, too, had considerable curiosity about the circus, for I gathered from Pansy's remarks that these exhibitions were one of the most important features of Purilian life. But of course, for the moment, everything else had to be subordinated to Pansy's crucial affairs.

As we drove into the town, the Presence (which apparently had accompanied us) obligingly remarked: 'Hillcrest, far removed from the bright lights and empty laughter of a jazz-mad age, is a quiet little town of homes.' And, indeed, the shaded street along which we were driving was lined with buildings which were unmistakably dwelling-houses. Children romped upon the ample lawns, and ever and again we caught glimpses of young and beautiful girls seated at pianos; of comely, well-coifed housewives singing merrily at their domestic tasks; and of sweet-faced, white-haired old ladies gathering roses in the warm, spring sunshine.

We drove at once to the building in which the lawyer had his office; a two-storey, wooden structure, in the principal street of the town. The lower story was occupied by a general provision store. We entered the building and mounted the rickety, ill-lighted staircase which gave access to the lawyer's office.

'Henry Billings,' remarked the Presence, as we opened the door, 'hadn't had a client since Blackstone was a pup.' It was not a promising introduction, nor was either the room or its occupant calculated to inspire confidence. The place was small and disorderly; everything was thickly covered with dust, and great cobwebs spread across the bookshelves (which I took to be a sign that the books had not been disturbed for some time.) And it seemed to me, too, that as we entered the room, several mice which had been nibbling the papers on Billings's desk, scurried to cover.

Billings, himself, was an oldish fellow, with baggy trousers and an unbuttoned vest. His hair was unkempt and rather too long, a fact which – had I not been a stranger in the country – should have put me on my guard against him, at once; for in Purilia such persons are almost always untrustworthy characters. I had the distinct impression that Billings had been awakened by our entrance. What made me think so was that, before addressing us, he rubbed his eyes, blinked, yawned several times, and shook himself violently, as though to throw off a heavy slumber.

Pansy explained the nature of her difficulties, exhibiting the riding-crop and the letter from the oil company as evidences of Millwood's duplicity. Billings examined the articles carefully, nodding gravely several times to indicate that he understood the situation. When Pansy had finished he removed a yellowed newspaper from a pile of law-books upon his desk and, blowing the dust off one of the books, became absorbed in its contents. I happened to glance at the newspaper's date-line and saw that it was twenty years old. Apparently the books had not been disturbed for twenty years! By now I was fully convinced that Billings's practice was not a very active one.

At length, Billings looked up from the book. 'I'll take the case,' he said, 'but first I must have a retainer.'

Pansy was thrown into consternation. She explained that she had no money; but the lawyer was adamant. At last in desperation, she took a gold circlet from her purse and proffered it to the lawyer.

'It's my mother's wedding-ring,' she said, with deep feeling; and then she added: 'It's the most precious thing I have in the world and you must promise to give it back to me.'

The ring (which suddenly assumed the dimensions of a wagon wheel) was a plain gold band and bore, I observed, the inscription: 'P. M. to H. M.' When the ring had shrunk again, Billings took it eagerly and slipped it into his pocket, assuring Pansy that it would be returned to her when the case was won. To this day, I cannot think of the appalling and unpredictable consequences of that simple act of Pansy's without a contraction of the heart! But, at the moment, it all seemed quite natural and inconsequential.

Our business with Billings concluded, we left his office, greatly cheered by his artful promises. Could we have but peered through the door that he shut behind us, our rejoicing would have given way to alarm, for we should have seen him gleefully rubbing his hands and smiling a crafty smile that spelled trouble for Pansy. And had we tarried a moment upon the stairs, we should have heard the unscrupulous wretch telephoning to Millwood and conspiring with him to bring about Pansy's discomfiture.

But we knew nothing of all this, and with light hearts we stepped out into the sunlight, ready for an afternoon's fun at the circus.

CHAPTER 6

WHEN we reached the pavement, we found that Jim, the hired man, was awaiting us, apparently none the worse for his mishap on the road. He was loitering outside the general provision store, smoking a cigarette, and as he saw us approaching I observed, to my horror, that he tossed the lighted cigarette into a barrel of gunpowder (which happened to be standing upon the pavement). The result was most disastrous. The barrel exploded violently, and poor Jim was tossed high into the air. Then, as he descended, he crashed bodily through the roof of the two-storey building into the premises occupied by a female dressmaking establishment where, at the moment of Jim's forcible entry, an elderly spinster was disrobing. Her consternation, at the sudden appearance of a man and in such a manner, may well be imagined!

Such, however, was the force of Jim's fall, that he splintered his way through the floor of the dressmaking establishment too, and plunged heavily into a barrel of molasses, in the provision store below. To make matters worse, the spinster, in her agitation, lost her footing, and followed Jim through the hole in the floor, falling head-first into a large open can of milk.

Horrified, we looked into the window of the store and saw the unfortunate Jim struggling out of the molasses barrel, while the merchant and his assistant, each holding one of the lady's legs, were trying to extricate her from the milk can, in which she was tightly wedged. At length, their efforts succeeded with unexpected suddenness, and as the lady bolted out of the milk can, her rescuers were catapulted violently backwards, the merchant into a vat of butter, and his assistant upon the sharp prongs of a garden rake.

The lady, her head streaming milk, now became painfully conscious of her semi-clothed state and hastened to seize a piece of sacking, with the intention of throwing it about her shoulders. It happened, however, that several crates of eggs were resting upon the sacking, so that when she pulled the cloth away the eggs crashed to the floor and were utterly demolished. As the merchant floundered out of the butter, and his assistant danced about in pain, Jim, who was groping about blindly, collided with the lady and, throwing his arms about her, embraced her heartily, so that she too became covered with molasses. Then, apparently becoming aware of the hostility of the others, he bolted out of the store and sped down the street, closely pursued by the lady and by the merchant and his assistant. Naturally all this tossing about had not been without its effect upon Jim's suspenders, and we observed that as he ran down the street he had great difficulty in keeping his trousers from falling. We were relieved, however, to see that all the persons concerned had escaped comparatively unhurt, from what might well have been a grave tragedy.

We made our way now to the circus-grounds, whither most of the townsfolk were proceeding. I looked with interest at the crowd that streamed toward the large tent, that had been pitched in the middle of a field, just outside the town. There were many pairs of happy young lovers, walking hand in hand, quite oblivious to the nods and smiles of their elders. And there were innumerable loving old couples too: quaint grey-beards and sweet-faced old ladies, reliving, no doubt, in this visit to the circus, the memories of their joyous youth. And, at the tent itself, numerous small boys were endeavouring by stealth or artifice to enter, without payment of the admission fee. The good-natured doorkeepers made a pretence of rebuffing the little fellows, but eventually permitted them to slip in.

As we were about to enter the tent, Johnson stopped suddenly. 'Listen,' he said, holding up his hand, 'I hear somebody crying.' We listened attentively and heard distinctly the sound of gentle weeping. With Johnson in the lead, we made our way around to the rear of the tent, where the performers had their quarters, and there, seated in the entrance to one of the smaller tents, we saw a young and beautiful girl, dressed in the silken tights and spangled skirts of a circus equestrienne.

There was no need to ask who she was or why she was weeping, for the Presence immediately announced: 'Mollie

St Clair, tired of circus life, after nineteen motherless years under the big top.'

As we gazed at her in pity, there floated by us the mirage of a rose-covered white cottage, very similar to the one in which Pansy dwelt. I had no doubt that this image was the projection of Mollie's wish. Weary of her nomadic life, I surmised, and of the empty plaudits of the crowd, she asked for nothing better than a quiet little home in the country.

She was too preoccupied with her sad thoughts to take notice of us. Then, all at once, she sprang to her feet in alarm, as an ill-favoured, black-moustached man, in the dress of a ringmaster, approached, whip in hand.

'George St Clair,' said the Presence, 'owner of the bankrupt show, put all the blame on his daughter's lack of interest.'

St Clair strode up to Mollie. 'The sheriff threatens to grab the show to-night,' he said, 'and if he does, I'll make you pay for it.'

'But, daddy dear,' said Mollie pleadingly, 'why couldn't we give up this life and settle down in a little house somewhere?'

By way of answer, the unfeeling brute raised his riding whip as though he were about to strike the cowering girl. But before he had an opportunity to carry out his intention, Johnson rushed forward and struck him a sharp blow on the right jaw. The astonished St Clair staggered back, with a nasty cut over his left eye, and Mollie turned to her rescuer, with a sweet smile of gratitude.

There is no telling what would have happened, if at that moment one of the circus attendants had not hurried up and announced that it was time for the entertainment to begin. St Clair, with an angry scowl at Johnson, and a muttered threat to Mollie, hastened off to the exhibition tent. Mollie pressed Johnson's hand, and as he walked with us to the exhibition tent it was easy to see that the lovely little artiste had taken possession of his fancy.

Near the entrance to the tent, a dozen clowns were awaiting their turn, and, as we lingered there for a moment, we accidentally witnessed a most pathetic incident. A messenger-boy hurried up and asked for one of the clowns by name. The possessor of the name was pointed out to him: an ageing man whose sad eyes belied his gay masquerade and painted grin. The boy handed him a telegram, and with trembling fingers the man tore open the message. He glanced at the contents, uttered a low cry, and staggered back, the yellow paper falling from his nerveless hand. I glanced at the telegram, which lay on the ground at my feet. It was a terse message informing him of the sudden death of his wife!

At that very moment, a sudden blare of horns gave the signal for the entrance of the clowns. Instantly, the afflicted man cast off the outward evidences of his grief, and, dashing the tears from his eyes, burst into a loud, cackling laugh and led his fellow merry-andrews into the arena, amid the merriment of the crowd. I subsequently learned that such incidents are of frequent occurrence in Purilia. The mortality rate among the relatives of circus folk and professional entertainers in general is appallingly high, and it is only by the cultivation of such stoicism as I have just described that these performers are able to pursue their careers.

We entered the tent now and were fortunate enough to find vacant places in the very front row. As I took my seat, I was surprised to see that my neighbour was none other than Henry Billings, the lawyer. He was accompanied by a be-spectacled elderly man, with a straggling growth of grey hair on his chin, and a large and very bright silver star on the lapel of his coat. Billings informed me that he was the attorney for the creditors of the circus and that his neighbour was the town sheriff (the star, which he polished continuously with his sleeve, being his emblem of office) whom he had instructed to take possession of the show, at the conclusion of the performance.

In the course of my conversation with Billings (whose

villainy in relation to Pansy's affairs I did not of course suspect) I acquired much detailed knowledge concerning these travelling circuses, with which, it can be truthfully said, Purilia is overrun. They are, I learned, always in financial difficulties – due, perhaps, to their excessive numbers. At any rate, Billings told me that he had never heard of one which could be deemed self-supporting.

I mentioned Mollie's dissatisfaction with circus life, and he assured me that this too is a most common phenomenon. In every one of these shows, I learned, there is at least one female performer who is weary of the itinerant life and eager to find an anchorage in some bucolic spot. Many of them, he said, actually forsake the circus to unite their lot with that of some village hotel proprietor or garage mechanic. I asked him how these marriages turn out, but he merely stared at me in blank uncomprehension and I did not pursue the inquiry. Indeed, it was only my ignorance of the customs of the country which had made me put the question, as the reader will see later, when I describe the Purilian institution of marriage.

It soon became obvious that the entertainment which we were watching was not a success. The performance was a listless and indifferent one and the applause was perfunctory. Even the lovely Mollie, balancing gracefully upon a milk-white horse, failed to arouse the enthusiasm of the crowd, although I need scarcely tell the reader that one pair of hands applauded vociferously.

But an unexpected incident suddenly changed the temper of the spectators. In the midst of a decidedly second-rate juggling turn, Jim burst into the arena, with a roaring lion at his heels! I could see, by the expression of the poor fellow's face, that he was in mortal terror; but the audience, taking this to be part of the show, burst into rapturous laughter and tumultuous applause.

A word of explanation is perhaps necessary. It seems that Jim, in attempting to elude his pursuers, had entered the circus grounds and, coming upon a cage which, for some unexplained reason, he assumed to be empty, he opened the door and took refuge within. Actually, however, the cage contained an unusually large and savage lion, and this beast, enraged by Jim's intrusion, emitted a frightful roar, which sent Jim flying out of the cage and into the exhibition tent, the lion hot upon his heels.

Around and around the arena they sped, Jim managing somehow to keep just out of the lion's reach. The circus folk, knowing the ferocious nature of the beast, were terrified. But the crowd howled its delight as Jim, his trousers slipping down, strove to outdistance the animal. At length, St Clair managed to entice the lion into a cage. Jim was saved, and what was more, his fortune was made, for his misadventure had turned the show from utter failure to triumphant success and the delighted St Clair offered the bewildered fellow a thousand dollars a week to repeat his act at each performance, which offer Jim, after some hesitation, accepted.

We hurried out of the tent to convey the good news to Mollie. But when we arrived at her little dressing tent there was no sign of her, and I could see that Johnson was troubled. His misgivings were confirmed a moment later when Mollie's maid, a faithful old Negress, appeared and gave him a note addressed to him in Mollie's hand.

Johnson read the note and silently passed it to us. 'I cannot bear this life any longer,' it said, 'and I am going away. Thank you for all your kindness. Good-bye and God bless you.' It was signed simply 'Mollie.'

We were too late! If only she had waited ten minutes more, she would have learned of the change in her father's fortune and all would have been well. But she was gone and there was no clue to her whereabouts. We questioned the maid, but either she did not know where the girl had gone, or else she could not be persuaded to divulge her knowledge.

Johnson was in despair and we could say nothing to lessen his grief. We made our way slowly back to the automobile and gloomily began our return journey to the Malone cottage. En route, we discussed the situation, speculating upon Mollie's probable destination. Pansy, who naturally could surmise far more readily than we the probable behaviour of a Purilian girl in such circumstances, was convinced that Mollie had gone to the city. And Johnson, determined to seize upon any thread, no matter how slender, announced his intention of proceeding to the metropolis next morning, in search of the lovely little circus performer, leaving me to assist Pansy in her difficulties with Millwood.

When we arrived at the Malone cottage, we found Mrs Malone standing at the gate, anxiously awaiting us, a letter in her hand. The letter was for Pansy, and Johnson and I went to our rooms, leaving her to read the missive. If only I had waited a moment before ascending the stairs! But how could I possibly have foreseen the contents of the letter or its effect upon Pansy?

I had been in my room scarcely five minutes, when I heard what seemed to be the sound of suppressed sobbing in Pansy's room, which adjoined mine. I listened intently for a few moments and then the sobbing ceased. With some hesitation, I went into the hall. The door of Pansy's room was half open, and, after knocking several times and receiving no reply, I ventured to enter.

The room was empty and its disordered state belied the habitual neatness and daintiness of its fair occupant. Bureau-drawers were open, clothing was scattered about, and a chair was overturned. In fact, everything indicated that Pansy had made a hurried exit. As I gazed about the room in bewilderment, I heard the sound of a motor below, and running to the window saw Pansy driving away from the house, a valise on the seat beside her. 'Pansy! Pansy!' I called. She heard me and turned upon me an enlarged and tear-stained face, upon which was written unutterable reproach. Then, without a word, or another look, she drove away.

I turned from the window, uncomprehendingly. Then my eye happened to fall upon a sheet of paper, which lay upon the floor. Mechanically, I picked it up and read it. It was the letter which had awaited Pansy upon our return from the town. 'I have just learned,' it said, 'that your fine friend is a crook. And what is more, he has a wife and two children.' It was signed 'Horace Millwood.'

Slowly, the situation dawned upon me. Clearly, what had happened was that Billings had betrayed us and that Millwood, seeing his scheme endangered, had taken this means of prejudicing Pansy against me.

But what surprised and pained me was that Pansy should have accepted unquestioningly this accusation of Millwood's. Not only did she know him to be utterly untrustworthy, but she might, I felt, have given me an opportunity to disprove his charges – which I could readily enough have done, since they had no foundation whatever in fact!

But, after a moment's reflection, I realized what an affront this dastardly accusation was upon Pansy's sweet maidenhood and how natural was her revulsion of feeling and her precipitate flight. That she had gone to the city, I had not the slightest doubt, and I determined to follow her at once, not only with a view to vindicating myself, but to prevent her from committing, in her distraction, some rash act.

I acquainted Johnson with what had happened and we decided to leave for the city at once, with a view to making a combined search for Mollie and Pansy. We went downstairs and confronted the gently reproachful face of Pansy's mother. With sorrowful firmness, she declined to listen to my explanation. 'I wouldn't have thought it of you,' she said, shaking her head sadly. 'I think you had better go.'

Dejectedly, we left the house and, as we turned a bend in the road, we caught a last glimpse of the cottage, with the figure of Mrs Malone standing in the doorway, her shawl about her stooped shoulders, her white head bent in sorrow.

We trudged along the road to the railway station. It was twilight, and along the very ridge of the distant hills a flock of sheep was making its way slowly in single file, their bodies silhouetted sharply against the sky. It was a lovely sight, but we were thinking of Pansy and of Mollie and our hearts were heavy.

CHAPTER 7

PERHAPS there are those among my readers who are of the opinion that I have allowed autobiographical details to bulk too largely in this account; and that I am offering them merely a personal narrative where they looked for a scholarly or, at any rate, a descriptive work. In extenuation, I can best say that it has seemed to me that a mere literal record of the remarkable occurrences which came under my notice, from the very moment of my arrival upon the Purilian scene, would enable the reader to form a clearer and more vivid image of that strange and remote land than I could hope to convey by offering him mere objective generalizations.

For the reader must bear in mind that the events which I have already recorded, extraordinary and improbable as they may seem, when judged by human and terrestrial criteria, represent a fair sample of the daily life of the average Purilian. Indeed, judged by Purilian standards, my first twenty-four hours in the country might be regarded as rather devoid of incident; and, all in all, the occurrences I have described may be fairly stated to be typical of the normal behaviour of the Purilians.

However, in the hope of illuminating such of these happenings as may seem to the reader inexplicable, and with a view, too, to making more credible the astounding events which I have yet to narrate, I shall set down here a few general observations concerning the inhabitants and the institutions of the country.

To begin with, if the reader wishes to derive from his contemplation of the Purilian scene something more than mere puzzlement, he must never forget for an instant that in Purilia there is the widest possible disparity between appearances and actualities. So that while, as I have already stated, Purilia in its external aspects bears a most startling resemblance to our own world, its essential characteristics are totally at variance with the realities of mundane life.

Architecturally and topographically, Purilian town and countryside are almost indistinguishable from their earthly counterparts. In physical appearance and in dress, the Purilians evidence many points of amazing resemblance to human beings. Even their language (as the judicious reader will have noted) is a variant of our own English tongue. But these likenesses are merely superficial. And one cannot spend even an hour in the country without a keen realization that he is in a world apart – a world which is the very antithesis of ours, a world dominated by alien, immutable laws, which transvalue all earthly values and create patterns unknown to the realm of terrestrial men and women.

The reader may recall that upon my first view of the country – before I had ever set foot upon its soil – I was astonished by the apparent absence of that intricate machinery of organized industrial production which in our own civilization confronts us at every turn. This first impression, further acquaintance with the country served to confirm, for Purilia, although possessing all the outward evidences of an intensively industrialized civilization, is, literally, almost without industries. What little mining there is, for example, is confined almost entirely to the unearthing of precious metals. Again, large manufacturing plants are practically non-existent. And indeed the few scattered mines and workshops serve not so much as industrial tools, but rather as convenient arenas for the emotional conflicts of their occupants.

The result of all this is that Purilia is happily free from all those disturbing social concomitants of large-scale industry which beset our less fortunate planet. Not only is there none of those bitter and protracted conflicts, between the employers and the employed, which periodically convulse our own social structure and bring misery and suffering to many thousands, but there is, properly speaking, no working class: no great social group absorbed in the necessary business of keeping body and soul together and engaged in an unremitting struggle against disease, accident, and advancing age.

One does, it is true, occasionally meet a worker. But these workers are almost invariably young and beautiful girls, as yet untouched by the ravages of industrialism and usually destined to escape from the industrial world, at an early age, by contracting a marriage with a young and handsome man of wealth. (Nor was I ever able to discover the exact nature of their occupation, for I found them always absorbed in the disentanglement of some emotional difficulty which seemed to occupy all their time and attention.) But of the great, grey plodding army of working-men and women which forms so large and important a part of our population, there is no sign in Purilia.

Poverty, it is true, exists; but it is, as I shall have occasion to point out later, a kind of poetic – almost idyllic – poverty, which ennobles and dignifies those who experience it. The dull, grinding, corroding poverty, which is perhaps the most universal and flagrant of human ills, is unknown in Purilia. There are no dismal slums in Purilia, no bread-lines, no workhouses, no shivering, undernourished bodies. Indeed, it can truthfully be said that almost all suffering is unknown in Purilia, except such suffering as finds a complete and happy cure in marriage, reconciliation, or reunion.

54

At the other end of the industrial scale, one encounters great magnates who, one learns, have amassed fabulous wealth in one or another form of industrial activity. But the exact nature of their operations I never quite succeeded in understanding. And in my numerous encounters with these men of affairs I always found them engaged in the furtherance or hindrance of some romantic alliance – often, I regret to say, in elaborate scheming to frustrate the happiness of their own children – to the complete neglect of their gigantic industrial enterprises. Now and then I did find one of them immersed in some incomprehensible but palpably fraudulent plot (or 'deal,' as these intrigues are called in Purilia) which always seemed to me quite incompatible with their position in the community and which bore no discernible relation to industry as it is known to us. In short, I was never able to penetrate the external evidence of industrial activity, and at last I was forced to the conclusion that there exists in Purilia only the appearance of industrialism, which no more requires an actual substantial basis than a wax flower requires soil and roots.

What is true of the industrial life of Purilia, is true also of its political life. There are vague external evidences of the existence of governmental agencies, but these too are mere appearances; actually the country is without political institutions. In consequence, the fortunate land is free from all those complex and perplexing problems of government and politics with which humans are only too familiar. Occasionally (as the reader will discover) one does meet an administrative officer; but these 'Governors', as they are called, have no other duty than the consideration of pleas for mercy, in behalf of prisoners who have been condemned to death.

Pursuing the inquiry further, one finds that most of the other multitudinous social problems which are ever-present in our own civilization are non-existent in Purilia. In matters of religion, the Purilians are a devout but not a bigoted people. Agnosticism and religious persecution are equally unknown. There is complete religious liberty and tolerance, unmarred by those distressing evidences of sectarianism which are for ever cropping out upon our planet. Indeed, it is generally recognized that religion is a matter for quiet, private observance and not for public debate; and, although one occasionally comes upon some pious person engaged in his devotions, the subject is never discussed, nor does it play any part in relationships between individuals.

Racial problems are happily absent, too. I do not mean that racial differences do not exist in Purilia, but merely that they do not create any of those ugly and distressing situations, amounting sometimes to actual conflict, of which we humans are only too well aware. Such racial difficulties as one finds in Purilia are military rather than social and are the result of occasional insurrections on the part of one or another of the dark-skinned races against the generally recognized and established supremacy of the whites. But these insurrections, as I shall have occasion to show, are always put down promptly and expeditiously – a small body of whites usually being able to put great numbers of dark-skinned rebels to speedy rout.

By now, I am sure the reader conceives Purilia as something of a Utopia and looks, perhaps with envy, upon the happy state of the Purilians, unperplexed and unharassed as they are by the bitter struggles, grinding cares, and confusing maladjustments which often make our terrestrial life well-nigh unbearable. And, in a measure, he is right. The Purilians are a simple, almost childlike people, who have reduced all life to a series of convenient symbols and easily comprehended gestures.

But, despite all this, I am by no means certain that a human being could live and thrive upon the Purilian sphere. For life in Purilia demands a degree of physical activity and an expenditure of emotional energy which, I am afraid, would overtax the stoutest human organism. The average

Purilian, in the course of a day, endures a series of escapades and physical adventures which at the end of a year at most would, I am certain, shatter the nervous constitution of the most robust man or woman.

As for the life of the emotions, it can almost be said that it comprises the whole range of Purilian life. What thought and work and play and simple relaxation are to us, emotional activity is to the Purilian. His life is a riot of emotional excess, one wave of intense feeling succeeding another, with bewildering and almost unbelievable rapidity. I doubt if any human could long endure the anguished suffering, the frenzied joy, and the transcendent love which are the substance of the Purilian's habitual regimen.

I spoke of love, and well I might, for love is perhaps the key to the whole Purilian world. Not such love as we know on earth: one dynamic element in our complex lives, with manifold biological, psychic, and aesthetic implications; but love as the be-all and end-all, love as the sole substance and meaning of life, love as a thing in itself, love universal and all-permeating, without any implication whatever. Such is love in Purilia; and an overpowering thing it is! And the reader must understand that the broad plains and the mountain-ranges, the quiet hill-sides and the pebbled beaches, the many-towered cities and the straggling towns, and the hordes of animate creatures who inhabit them, are but the paraphernalia of this eternal, cosmic love.

The reader will now, I hope, be able to understand the interesting caste system, which is one of the most remarkable features of the Purilian social order. There are at least five well-defined castes in Purilia, and I shall endeavour to acquaint the reader with the distinguishing characteristics of each.

The most venerated, although by no means the largest of these social classes, is the Umbilican caste. Pansy's mother, Mrs Malone, was a member of this caste, and the description of her physical appearance, which I have already given, includes most of the characteristics by which persons belonging to this caste are recognizable. Only mothers may belong to the Umbilican caste and only mothers who have suffered deeply – but since in Purilia motherhood and suffering are almost synonymous, nearly any mother is eligible (provided she is sufficiently advanced in years and not too tall; greatness of stature in a mother being regarded as reprehensible).

It is impossible to exaggerate the esteem in which the Umbilicans are held throughout the length and breadth of Purilia (always excepting, of course, the territories occupied by the dark-skinned races). In fact, while Christianity is the nominal and established religion of the country, the religious emotion of the people finds its happiest expression in mother-worship, and the Umbilicans have a status which can truly be characterized as priestlike or even semi-divine. An Umbilican can do no wrong, and the suggestion that she can corresponds to blasphemy among us. Indeed, in the absence of formal political institutions, upon which I have already commented, the government of the country may best be described as a matriarchate, the authority of the Umbilicans being in no way diminished by the fact that they abhor self-assertiveness and spend their lives in self-abnegation and perpetual sorrowing.

It must be explained that maternity in Purilia is in no sense a biological function, but is solely emotional and spiritual. I shall have occasion to refer again to the vexatious problem of the origin of life in Purilia, but, for the present, it is merely necessary that the reader understand that the relationship between an Umbilican and her children is a metaphysical rather than a physical one.

One of the many curious paradoxes which one encounters in the course of one's inquiries into the mysteries of Purilian love is that although the Umbilicans, as I have said, are literally worshipped by all and sundry, especially of course by their children, these children, nevertheless, are constantly guilty of conduct which, they can scarcely fail to recognize, must have the effect of aggravating the venerated parents' already heavy load of anguish. In fact, it is a matter of almost everyday occurrence for some youth or maiden to leave the maternal home without leaving a single clue to his or her whereabouts, and to remain away for months or even years without making the slightest effort to communicate with the distressed Umbilican!

The lives of the Umbilicans are simple and uneventful, even by earthly standards. Weeping, knitting, and prolonged contemplation of the portraits or photographs of their absent children comprise almost the whole range of their activities. Sometimes, they engage in two, or even all three, of these occupations simultaneously, and occasionally, in their lighter moments, they turn their attention to the concoction of fruit pasties – an art in which they are unexcelled. But, on the whole, their lives are monotonous and unenlivened, and, although one cannot but admire their saintliness, one can scarcely regard their lot as an enviable one. In fact, for me, the deep sorrow occasioned by the demise of one of these admirable creatures was always tempered by the consoling reflection that she had found, at last, surcease from her abiding woe.

Ranking only slightly below the Umbilicans, are the Pudencians, a large and thriving caste. The Pudencians are young and beautiful girls ranging in age from eighteen to twenty-two. They are usually blonde, although occasionally one with dark tresses is encountered. The essential and distinguishing characteristic of this caste is virginity, and it is this quality which accounts for the exalted position which the Pudencians occupy in the Purilian social system.

It may strike the uninformed reader as paradoxical that, in a land in which maternity is invested with religious sanctity, virginity also is elevated to a plane almost equally exalted. But, actually, there is no inconsistency here, although I confess it is difficult to make this clear to a human who has never visited Purilia. I can perhaps best elucidate this difficult matter by explaining that in Purilia virginity, like maternity, is symbolical and metaphysical, rather than biological or physical. The two castes are entirely distinct; there is no progression from one to the other: that is to say, it is unthinkable that an Umbilican was ever a Pudencian or that a Pudencian is a potential Umbilican. Indeed, it would be in the nature of sacrilege to suggest that a Pudencian is capable of maternity, or that an Umbilican, in achieving maternity, surrendered her virginity. The two states are altogether disparate: the function of the Umbilicans is to be mothers, that of the Pudencians is to be virgins.

I know, only too well, that more than one reader will find himself dissatisfied with so inadequate an explanation. But, unfortunately, it is the best that I can offer. The whole subject is surrounded in Purilia with a kind of reverential mystery, which it is almost impossible to penetrate. As for the question of birth, which of course is closely related to this discussion, I must admit that I succeeded in learning almost nothing about it.

Here we have the most striking illustration of how deceptive are the outward physical resemblances between the Purilians and ourselves. Actually, the whole life process is totally dissimilar. And while it is impossible for me to say what birth in Purilia is, I can say quite authoritatively what it is not. It is not, then, the result of sexual union. Indeed, a Purilian would be profoundly horrified by any such suggestion – assuming that he could be made to understand it!

But lest the reader assume from this that Purilian birth is a sort of parthenogenesis, I must hasten to add that, while birth is never the result of sexual conjugation, it is invariably the result of marriage. In other words, Purilian children do have fathers as well as mothers; and, although the fathers are held in little esteem, they apparently fulfil some necessary, if altogether inscrutable, function in the perpetuation of Purilian life.

My own inference – and I confess that it is nothing more

than a conjecture – is that there is some generative principle inherent in the marriage ceremony which, in some unknown way, eventually produces Purilian infants. I base this largely upon the fact that, in Purilia, there is no birth outside of wedlock. This, I think, argues that the procreative function inheres in the marriage institution rather than in the physiological constitution of the parties to the marriage.

This view is supported by the fact that babies are really not born, but merely occur. There is no long and difficult period of gestation. No one, in Purilia, has ever seen a woman who gave outward evidence of approaching maternity. There are no lying-in hospitals, no obstetricians, no midwives. Purilian mothers are happily spared all the hazards and the pangs that attend human birth. Often, indeed, the arrival of the little one comes as something of a surprise to the parents. A pair is joined in wedlock, and then, after a while, a baby appears, usually well-developed and fully clothed. Occasionally, the mother has vague premonitions of the arrival of the infant and, sometimes, even goes to the length of preparing a garment or two for the expected child; but this practice is not regarded with favour, and is generally looked upon as unwomanly and indelicate.

What makes the whole situation even more involved and obscure is that although marriage can by no means be said to entail loss of virginity, entrance into the marital state automatically deprives a Pudencian of her caste. And yet, despite this, the sole end which every Pudencian has in view (and which she invariably achieves) is marriage. Let the reader resolve for himself this tangle of paradoxes! I can do no more than acquaint him with the facts.

One hypothetical explanation of the eagerness of the Pudencians to enter the marital state is that they are seeking an escape from the exacting and frequently perilous mode of life which they invariably lead. For, unlike the Umbilicans, the Pudencians lead lives of unremitting physical activity and emotional stress. On the one hand, they are the objects of unrelenting persecution by the Vauriens (a despicable caste, to which I shall have occasion to refer again) who endeavour, by fraud, force, or stealth, to engage the Pudencians in disastrous and dishonourable alliances or, more often to do them actual physical violence – and when I say physical, I mean, of course, metaphysical – and, on the other hand, they are harrowed by an unending succession of enforced separations and devastating misunderstandings between themselves and the members of another caste, known as the Paragonians, who are always the rightful possessors of the affections of the Pudencians.

So perhaps it is not to be wondered that a Pudencian should willingly, even eagerly, sacrifice the enormous prestige which her caste gives her, to embrace the serene obscurity of marriage. For in marriage, a Pudencian finds refuge from the threats and machinations of the Vauriens. Safe in the arms of some handsome Paragonian, she sinks into a tranquil security, and – as I shall have occasion to relate – fades gracefully from the turmoils of the Purilian scene. Indeed, a marriage in Purilia has about it a finality which is almost lethal, and in most cases the sorely tried Pudencian finds in it a restful physical obliteration and an eternity of disembodied happiness. For in Purilia the dream of human poets has become a reality and marriage is the apotheosis of spiritual love. (I write this, in the fullness of after-knowledge. For during my sojourn in the country I was unable to penetrate the mystery in which the subject is veiled.)

A word or two more about the Pudencians. They are invariably kind, sweet-tempered, and sympathetic. Their behaviour is the quintessence of womanly modesty. They do not drink or smoke, or indulge in any of the other manifold improprieties to which so many young women upon our planet are addicted. They are quick to resent any male attention which does not contemplate marriage; and, while their lives are literally conditioned by love, they hold themselves superior to passion, and the essential purity of their nature makes it impossible for them ever to lend themselves to those crude outward manifestations of love with which we sensual earthlings are only too familiar. What makes their conduct all the more admirable is that, more often than not, they seek careers upon the stage or in other departments of the amusement world where, as everyone knows, conditions are most unfavourable to the preservation of female innocence and modesty. Yet, despite – or because of – these self-imposed handicaps, they triumphantly maintain that militant purity which is traditional to their caste.

Another Pudencian trait, worthy of notice, is the meticulous neatness of these lovely girls. Neither shipwreck, nor battle, nor all-night vigil can dim for an instant their luscious bloom or ruffle a single strand of their tasteful coiffures. Indeed, I have known a Pudencian to emerge from a flooded mine or a shell-torn front-line trench – whither she had gone on some characteristic errand of mercy – with her lovely face as blooming and her frock as dainty and unruffled as though she had just stepped out of her boudoir. It is as though there were, about these Pudencians, an aura of purity and of modish loveliness which is capable of withstanding any disaster or woe.

(Perhaps the reader will understand more clearly now Pansy's precipitate flight and her credulous acceptance of Millwood's accusations. The very guilelessness and innocence of these girls make it impossible for them to suspect others of deceit, and, at the same time, make them take alarm at anything that might conceivably be construed as an evidence of duplicity on the part of those whom they love and trust. But no one who has not had the happiness of knowing a Pudencian can fully understand her sensitive nature.)

The Paragonians are, to all outward appearances, the male counterparts of the Pudencians. Like the Pudencians, they are young and handsome. They, too, are concerned chiefly in contracting a marriage, in which they will find blissful obliteration. And, indeed, the achievement of this end is a career so arduous in its nature that anyone but a Paragonian would shrink from it. Not only does the courtship of a Pudencian involve the most agonizing emotional complications, but usually, before the union can be consummated, the aspiring Paragonian must undergo a sort of ordeal by battle, in the course of which he runs the most frightful risks and performs almost Herculean feats of strength and skill.

Fortunately, the Paragonians are all trained athletes, expert horsemen and marksmen, skilled aviators, untiring swimmers, and clever boxers, and swordsmen. To these attainments, they add indomitable courage and unflagging resourcefulness, so that it is not to be wondered that they emerge triumphantly from every situation. They are apparently immortal and invincible; at any rate, there is no record of a Paragonian's death or defeat. A Paragonian is easily a match for six or eight white-skinned adversaries and twenty or thirty dark-skinned ones. And, while the Paragonian may occasionally sustain severe injuries and even frightful wounds, there is some curative quality in his physical constitution which makes for a miraculously speedy recovery, without disfiguring scars.

The Paragonians, like the Pudencians, are scrupulously neat, and somehow always manage, even in the thick of battle, to shave smoothly and to gloss their hair. Indeed, spiritual love and tidiness are the two great bonds which make inevitable the union of Pudencians and Paragonians. Like the Pudencians too, the Paragonians bear a striking resemblance to each other, and during my sojourn in Purilia I was constantly thrown into confusion by my inability to distinguish the members of the respective castes, one from another.

The Vauriens, to whom I have already referred, are a numerous and flourishing caste, despite the heavy casualties which they constantly suffer. They are a powerful order, but, as they employ their power only for evil ends, they are rightfully despised. They too, like all the other Purilian castes, are conditioned solely by love. But while the love of the Vauriens is certainly not spiritual love, it is difficult to say just what it is. In some ways, it resembles physical love, but since that is unknown in Purilia I can describe this strange emotion of the Vauriens only as symbolic lust. It is always aroused by a Pudencian, but, since no Vaurien has ever been successful in his designs, it is impossible to say what would happen if he were.

The traditional lack of success of the Vauriens does not, in the least, deter them from a continuance of their pursuit of the Pudencians. And this pursuit, together with the physical combats with some Paragonian which it always involves, constitutes the substance of a Vaurien's life.

The Vauriens fall roughly into two classes: the white-skinned and the dark-skinned. (I need scarcely say that all Umbilicans, Pudencians, and Paragonians are white-skinned.) The white-skinned Vauriens are usually distinguishable by their moustaches and derby hats, and their habit of smoking cigars. They have no fondness for children or animals and often treat both with distinct unkindness. But chiefly they are recognizable by the looks which they cast upon the Pudencians – looks which to the initiated observer palpably disavow spiritual love.

The dark-skinned Vauriens are usually bearded and almost always wear some bizarre garment, in lieu of the trousers of civilization and probity. Indeed, I had not been long in Purilia before I learned to associate strangeness of attire with duplicity, and, before many days, I did not have to be told that a man who spurned trousers could be up to no good. But the reader will learn in good time of my actual encounters with the Vauriens!

One caste remains to be described: the Bordellians, who bear much the same relationship to the Vauriens that the Pudencians bear to the Paragonians. The Bordellians are, almost invariably, dark-haired, plump, and past the first flush of youth. They are the lowest of all the Purilian castes and have almost the status of the untouchables in our own India. Umbilicans and Pudencians shrink from them in horror; and this sentiment is shared by the Paragonians too, despite the fact that they are sometimes temporarily distracted by the wiles of the Bordellians.

It is difficult to convey to the reader the disesteem and loathing in which these repulsively attractive females are held. They spend their lives in attempting to lure Paragonians, although to what they wish to lure them I never succeeded in discovering. Spiritual love is unknown to them, nor do they possess virginity. On the other hand, it cannot be said that they have ever surrendered their virginity; at least no one in Purilia would ever admit that such was the case, and I finally arrived at the conclusion that virginity is simply a quality which they had never, at any time, possessed. This, too, will be difficult for the terrestrial reader to understand; but he must bear in mind that I am writing of a people who inhabit a sphere so remote from ours that it would be impossible even to convince them of our existence.

Naturally, most of what I have written is the summarized result of months of painstaking investigation. I have introduced it at this point in my narrative, because I feel that, without some familiarity with the conditions of Purilian life, the amazing happenings which I have yet to record would be utterly incomprehensible to the reader.

And now let us return to the quest for Pansy and Mollie upon which Johnson and I were engaged.

CHAPTER 8

As we drew near the little way-station, we heard the whistle of an approaching locomotive, and, surmising that the train was bound for the city, we quickened our pace in an effort to catch it. When we arrived at the station, we were relieved to see that the train was just rounding a curve, into sight. (I should explain that, in Purilia, trains are always rounding curves. Although there are vast areas of lowland and prairie, there is nowhere, throughout the entire country, as much as a mile of straight track. My ignorance of engineering makes it impossible for me to explain this curious method of railroad construction.)

But, as the train thundered on without slackening its speed, we surmised that it did not stop at the little station. 'Let's try to make it,' shouted Johnson; and running after the flying train, we managed to board it just as it was rounding a curve, out of sight.

Several indignant conductors and trainmen confronted us, and for a moment it seemed their intention to throw us bodily from the speeding train. But, when we had explained the gravity of our errand, they became most sympathetic and co-operative and not only allowed us to remain on the train, but provided us with berths in one of the sleeping-cars.

The car to which we were assigned was similar in appearance to the Pullman sleeping-cars, familiar to American travellers. We were interested to note that our fellow-occupants of the car were members of a travelling circus (although not, of course, the St Clair troupe). In addition to a beautiful young Pudencian, whose face bore evidences of some deep sorrow, there was a number of those anatomical monstrosities known as 'freaks'. These included a giant eight feet tall, and a dwarf scarcely four, a woman of incredible bulk, and another, whose face was adorned with an enormous bristling beard.

As the Negro porter (whose name, we learned subsequently, was George) was engaged in preparing the berths for the night, we made our way to the platform, at the rear end of the train, in hope of making some observations, which would increase our knowledge of the country. And, indeed, we were not disappointed, for the journey proved to be a most eventful one.

For a time, we were interested in observing a number of pursuits, upon the road which ran parallel to the tracks. Sometimes it was a Vaurien who was pursuing a Pudencian; sometimes it was a Paragonian who was pursuing a Vaurien who held a Pudencian in unwilling custody; sometimes it was a Vaurien or a band of Vauriens who pursued a Paragonian, accompanied or unaccompanied by a Pudencian. There seemed to be no rule about it, except that, when a Pudencian figured in the chase at all, it was always as the pursued and never as the pursuer.

But, now and again, our attention was diverted from the exciting happenings on the road. Once, we were surprised to see two police officers pursuing a bandit, along the tops of the cars of an express train that roared by, in the opposite direction. As the officers drew nearer to the bandit, who was leaping boldly from car to car, the desperado turned and fired. One of the officers staggered and fell, to what must have been a certain death. But as the other, who was obviously a Paragonian and therefore invulnerable, continued the pursuit, the bandit suddenly grasped the branch of a tree which happened to overhang the railroad track, and swung himself off the train, just as it rounded a curve. Without a moment's hesitation, the Paragonian seized the swaying branch and followed the bandit into the tree; and, as our train rounded a curve, I saw the two engaged in a desperate hand-to-hand struggle, in the topmost branches of the tree.

A little farther on, we saw the appalling results of what apparently had been a head-on collision between two passenger trains. The scene, of course, was one of almost hopeless confusion; but, nevertheless, we managed to catch glimpses of several stirring and moving incidents; as for example, a tall Paragonian emerging from the flaming wreckage with the unconscious form of a Pudencian slung over his shoulder. The flames had evidently torn his shirt to shreds, but otherwise he seemed unharmed. The girl, whose face loomed suddenly before us, now slowly opened her eyes; and we could hear her say faintly, 'What has happened? Where am I?'

Near by, seated among the debris, was another lovely Pudencian, clad in the freshly laundered uniform of a trained nurse. In her lap, she held the head of a Paragonian, who seemed in desperate need of medical attention. Accordingly, I was a little surprised to see the girl bend forward and press her lips to those of the unconscious youth (for I did not know at the time that, in Purilia, spiritual love is a most efficacious remedy for physical, as well as mental, ills). Almost instantly, the young man opened his eyes and, as our train rounded a curve, I heard him say faintly, 'Where am I? What has happened?'

I learned, later, that the pair were lovers, who had been separated, some months before, by the failure of a letter to arrive. The girl, believing herself betrayed, had taken up nursing, and a fortunate chance had drawn her to the spot where the train, in which her lover was journeying to the city to look for her, had been wrecked.

If the train had not been wrecked, he would, of course, have continued on his way to the city and it is conceivable that he and his sweetheart would never have met again. But it is characteristic of Purilian disasters that one always finds in them mitigating circumstances and that almost invariably, in the midst of carnage, flame, and wreckage, justice triumphs and fond hearts are reunited. And, while the human may be shocked by the havoc wrought by these often easily preventable disasters, the Purilian feels that, after all, a little damaged property and a few maimed bodies are a small price to pay for the triumph of spiritual love.

When we returned to our sleeping-car, rather wearied as a result of witnessing so many harrowing incidents, we found that the circus folk were preparing to retire. The dwarf had been assigned (rather inconsiderately, I thought) to an upper berth, and as he could not, of course, climb up unaided, the giant obligingly seized him by the back of the neck, and lifted him bodily into the berth. The stout lady, too, had been allotted an upper berth, and, just as we entered the car, we saw the little ladder, which she had been trying to climb, splinter under her weight, causing the poor lady to fall heavily upon a large valise, which happened to be standing in the aisle. She was assisted to her feet by the concerted efforts of five or six of her fellow travellers. Fortunately, she was unhurt, but the valise upon which she had fallen was completely demolished and a dozen golf-balls, which it happened to contain, were crushed into mere flat disks. The indignation of the owner of the valise could be easily deduced from his excited shouts and frantic gesticulations.

The Negro porter, George, was now called upon to assist the lady to ascend to her berth. He managed to procure, from the fireman, a stout iron ladder, and with the aid of this the lady made a second attempt. The iron rungs of the ladder, however, bent beneath her weight, and when she reached the top rung, it was impossible for her to climb into the berth. At this point, George came to her aid and, putting his shoulder beneath the lady's ample haunches, heaved manfully. It was no easy task and his eyes rolled wildly with the agony of his efforts, while enormous globules of sweat appeared upon his forehead. At length, with one last desperate lunge, he succeeded in hurling the lady into the berth, which – solid steel though it was – sagged dangerously beneath her bulk. The onlookers laughed merrily, as the exhausted porter fell limply to the floor, and I was happy to note that a smile lighted even the pensive face of the little Pudencian.

This incident concluded, I retired to my own berth and was just falling off to sleep, when I was startled by a frightful uproar which suddenly broke out in the car. I quickly thrust my head between the curtains to ascertain what had happened. The whole car was in a state of turmoil and confusion, but for some time I could not discover what was wrong. Then, suddenly, I saw George, the Negro porter, his face contorted with terror, rushing down the aisle, pursued by a enormous gorilla. It seems that this animal (which was one of the attractions of the circus) had somehow managed to escape from the baggage-car in which it was being transported, and had made its way to our sleeping-car.

The sight of the gorilla (which, I noted, was much more manlike in appearance than any of the species that I have seen upon our planet) was, of course, enough to throw the occupants of the car into a state of terror. Much aimless running about ensued, with resultant collisions among the half-dressed occupants of the berths. As for the wretched porter, so frenzied was he by fright that he dived heedlessly through one of the car windows to what must have been a certain death, for the train was moving with terrific speed.

In the confusion, the gorilla managed, somehow, to disappear, and his trainer, who by this time had arrived upon the scene, began a frantic search for the animal. In this he was aided by the giant, who, it seems, was greatly concerned about the safety of the dwarf, the two being devoted friends and inseparable companions. Bewildered and greatly worried, the giant did not notice that the dwarf was dodging in and out between his lengthy legs, and, mistaking in the confusion the location of the dwarf's berth, the tall fellow thrust his head into the berth occupied by the stout lady. Outraged by what she regarded as an affront upon her womanhood, the adipose female screamed indignantly, and, lunging forward at the intruder, unfortunately lost her balance and tumbled into the aisle, falling with all her weight upon a valise, containing several bottles of intoxicants, which happened to be standing there. The resultant alcoholic deluge can well be imagined; and several of the travellers, forgetting their fears, bent down and eagerly scooped up handfuls of the escaping liquor, which they consumed with great relish.

Meanwhile, the gorilla's trainer, having somehow arrived at the belief that his charge had concealed itself in a certain lower berth, thrust his hand between the curtains and, encountering a hairy object, tugged at it triumphantly, assuming that he had captured the missing animal. Indignant female shrieks soon disillusioned him, for it seems that the berth in question was occupied by the bearded lady, and the trainer had inadvertently seized hold of the poor woman's whiskers!

There is no telling what would have happened if, at this moment, the fugitive ape had not been discovered seated in another berth, placidly munching a banana. It seems that the berth was occupied by a fruit-vendor, who was carrying with him a large hamper full of luscious bananas. The huge beast, unhappy in his confinement in the baggage-car, and dreaming perhaps of his native jungle, had somehow sensed the presence of the fruit and had made his way to the sleeping-car in quest of it. He had no intention of harming anyone, and, having by this time made an ample meal, he allowed himself to be removed from the prostrate body of the fruit-vendor, upon which he was seated, and accompanied his trainer docilely back to the baggage-car. We all returned to our berths now, without further incident, except that the fat lady fell heavily, several times, as a result of slipping upon the banana-skins which the gorilla had scattered about the car.

But my head had scarcely touched the pillow before the train came to a sudden stop, with a violence that almost threw me out of my berth. I sprang up and, hastily throwing on a few articles of clothing, stepped out into the aisle, which was now filled with excited fellow passengers. No one seemed to know just what had happened; but, suddenly, the slender figure of a man appeared at the end of the car. He held a revolver in each hand, and the lower part of his face was concealed by a black silk handkerchief. It was obvious that he was a train-robber. The women shrieked hysterically, but, with a frightful oath, the bandit ordered them to be quiet and then, in hard threatening accents, commanded us all to throw up our hands.

Two other robbers, much more burly than the first, now appeared and proceeded to search the berths for valuables, while the first continued to threaten us with his revolvers. The robbers conducted their search with what seemed to me needless violence, tossing the clothing of the passengers about and even trampling upon it. The young Pudencian (whose name it seems was June) drew tightly about her throat the long coat which she had thrown over her night apparel. A sudden expansion of her features gave me an excellent opportunity to observe the mortal terror which they reflected.

While the robbers were collecting their loot, one of them suddenly held up a huge gold band, which he had found in one of the berths, exclaiming: 'Hey, Jack, look at the solid gold dog-collar.' He was answered by an indignant shriek from the stout lady. 'Give me that, you big crook,' she screamed. 'That's my wedding-ring!' Despite the gravity of the situation, and the poor lady's outraged sensibilities, the other passengers could not refrain from laughter.

The robbers now approached June, who cowered visibly. The larger of the two thrust his face close to hers and then, noticing a gold chain about her neck, harshly commanded her to give it to him. June pleaded to be allowed to retain the chain, but the heedless ruffian tore open the girl's coat at the throat, without regard to her maidenly modesty, and snatched the chain from her neck. I saw now that a simple gold locket was suspended from the chain.

'Please don't take my locket,' pleaded the girl. 'My sweetheart's picture is in it.'

At the sound of her voice, the young bandit staggered, as though he had been struck. Forgetting the necessity of keeping the passengers at bay, he lowered his revolvers and hurried forward to where June and his two companions stood. 'Let me see that locket,' he said in a rough voice, snatching it unceremoniously from his fellow bandit's hand. As he opened it, its swollen interior revealed the photograph of a young and handsome man.

The young bandit's agitation was obvious. 'You say this is your sweetheart?' he asked the girl in harsh tones.

'Yes, sir,' replied the girl, her eyes filling with tears. 'He went away, and it's all I have to remember him by.'

'Then you are not engaged to Sir Cecil Montmorency?' asked the young man, who was evidently profoundly moved.

'No,' said the girl, her face revealing her horror of Sir Cecil. 'I hate him. I have never loved anyone but Jack.'

At these words, the young bandit tore the silk handkerchief from his face.

'Jack!' exclaimed June, in mingled wonder and delight. And indeed, the youthful bandit proved to be none other than the young and handsome man whose photograph the locket contained!

Explanations naturally followed. It seems that Jack and June had been betrothed, some months before, June preferring the penniless youth to the wealthy Sir Cecil. The latter, however (who was the last of a noble but degenerate line) had resolved to have the girl at any cost. To achieve this end, he had addressed an anonymous letter to Jack informing him that June was secretly engaged to Sir Cecil.

Upon receiving this false intelligence, Jack's grief had known no bounds. Embittered and disillusioned by what he believed to be the faithlessness of his sweetheart, he had left home without informing anyone of his whereabouts, and, made cynical by despair, had determined to prey upon the society of which theretofore he had been a useful member. Making the acquaintance of a band of train-robbers, he fell in with them and before long, by virtue of his daring courage, became their leader.

June, meanwhile, heart-broken by what she regarded as her lover's desertion, had joined a circus, partly in the hope of encountering him in the course of her wandering, and partly because she believed that in the world of sawdust and canvas she might find forgetfulness.

Now, as a result of the fortuitous meeting I have described, everything was happily adjusted. Jack, his faith in June completely restored and eager to take his place again in the world of honest men, not only announced his intention of giving up his life of banditry, but compelled his two companions to restore to the other passengers all the valuables which they had appropriated. Some of the passengers demanded that the two robbers be placed under arrest, but this Jack would not allow. 'They may be crooks,' he said, 'but they've been good pals to me, and I never go back on a pal.' And even the most vindictive of the passengers could not but applaud this admirable sentiment. The two robbers shook hands heartily with Jack and June, wishing them the greatest happiness, and intimating that Jack's splendid example would probably have the effect of causing them, too, to give up their life of crime. These ceremonies concluded, the two robbers took their departure.

At this moment, a man of dignified appearance, who until now had been silent, stepped forward and announced that he was the district attorney and that it was his painful duty to place Jack under arrest. The happiness of the reunited pair immediately gave way to the darkest despair.

But now, an elderly man, who had also been silent, stepped forward and greeted the district attorney. He proved to be not only a lifelong friend of both the district attorney and Jack's father (lately deceased) but the president of a large bank as well. He had been most favourably impressed by Jack's splendid behaviour and he now asked the district attorney to overlook the boy's offences, which, as he pointed out, had been due to grief and not to an evil nature. He added that he was willing to give the lad an important position in his banking establishment, which would assure the happy future of the young pair.

The district attorney hesitated for a moment, and then his humaneness triumphed over his sense of official responsibility. Placing one hand upon June's shoulder, and the other upon Jack's, he said to the boy, in paternal accents: 'I guess this little girl needs you more than the law does.' The despair of the young couple now gave way once more to unbounded happiness, and as Jack took the lovely girl in his arms, the district attorney informed them that Sir Cecil had been arrested that morning, in connexion with some land frauds, and that he undoubtedly faced a long prison term.

The conductor of the train, who had been watching this scene with much interest, now asked if the train might proceed, as it was already more than an hour late. Jack joyfully told him to go ahead, and I retired to my berth, utterly exhausted by the exciting events of the day. The rest of the journey was without incident, and I slept soundly, until I was awakened by the Presence's bland announcement: 'The rising sun finds the travellers arrived in the great city.'

CHAPTER 9

As Johnson and I stepped out of the railroad station, into a street thronged with vehicles and pedestrians, the Presence declaimed (for our edification, no doubt) : 'The city of steel towers – a modern Babylon, where men and women, in their frantic struggle for wealth and fame, sometimes forget God.'

Scarcely had these words been uttered, when there whirled rapidly before our dazzled vision a bewildering series of glimpses of teeming metropolitan life. Serrated sky-lines; great avenues black with traffic; a lofty cathedral; the interior of a vast and luxurious restaurant; a street lined with theatres; a huge office buzzing with hundreds of busy

76

clerks; a dozen mighty ships at anchor; a colossal stadium crammed with cheering thousands; the whirring presses of a great newspaper; a mass-meeting in a public square – all these swirled before our startled eyes and left us with the unmistakable impression that here, indeed, was a large city, in which things were done upon a grand scale.

But there were less grandiose glimpses too, which served to convince us that the city was not without its more intimately human aspects. A police officer directing the traffic, with what seemed a needless expenditure of energy; a structural steel-worker perched precariously hundreds of feet above the roaring street; an obviously wealthy but rather overdressed lady stepping haughtily into a limousine; an anaemic little shop-girl carrying an oversized hatbox; a sensual-looking clubman eating caviare; a workman in overalls eating bread and cheese; a group of important-looking men seated about a conference table; a washer-woman bending wearily over her tub; a beautiful diva soulfully singing an aria; and a little golden-haired child, oblivious to the hurrying passers-by, happily fondling a tiny kitten – these vignettes, impinging themselves upon us in rapid succession, could scarcely fail to persuade us that metropolitan life is indeed varied and abounding in sharp contrasts. But my subsequent investigations taught me that there is really much less variety in Purilian urban life than appears at first glance.

Having learned that there was an excellent hotel not far from the railroad station, we decided to make our way there on foot in order to become better acquainted with the characteristics of the city. (I may say, in passing, that the perils attendant upon vehicular travel in Purilia always made me prefer to go on foot, whenever it was possible.)

We were struck, at once, by the great number of florists' and jewellers' establishments. In fact, retail commerce in a Purilian city is confined almost exclusively to shops of this kind. Their patronage is almost entirely male. In every florist shop, we saw both Paragonians and Vauriens busily making purchases. We observed that while the Paragonians seemed to prefer roses and violets, the Vauriens showed no interest in anything but orchids.

The jewellery shops play a most important part in Purilian life. They do a thriving trade in engagement rings and wedding-rings, and we saw more than one Paragonian stop short to gaze at the display of wedding-rings, which the windows of these shops always contain, and then, as though suddenly inspired, hurry into the shop to purchase one of the little talismans.

In addition to these emblems of betrothal and marital union, the shops carry a large stock of costly and pretentious jewels. Most of these gems have strange and often sanguinary histories, many of them having been torn from the foreheads of exotic idols. They are usually of quaint design and exquisite workmanship and their effect upon the character of the Purilians is most debilitating, the desire to possess them often being the direct cause of the most revolting crimes.

I am convinced that one of the most needed reforms in Purilia is the restriction of the jewellery trade to engagement and wedding-rings. As long as the present uncontrolled traffic in precious stones is permitted to continue, the task of checking the appalling lawlessness from which the country suffers is a hopeless one. But any attempt at such a reform would undoubtedly meet with the organized opposition of the Vaurien caste and would certainly be doomed to defeat.

The Presence apprised us of our arrival at our hotel by remarking: 'The Metropolis Hotel, a palatial hostelry, where the idle rich pass their days and nights in wasteful luxury, mindless of the suffering of the toiling millions.'

With the assistance of some seven or eight liveried attendants, we entered the great doors of the hotel and found ourselves in a rotunda which in size compared favourably with the interior of the Church of St Peter in Rome. Great columns soared to incredible heights, and the eye lost itself in vistas which faded dimly away in the remote distance. Potted palms, marble fountains, great tapestries, thick carpets, and furniture of rather alarming dimensions, all contributed to an impression of expenditure upon a lavish scale. Nor was this impression belied by the spectacle of scores of hurrying flunkeys in resplendent uniforms, and hundreds of men and women, whom I took to be guests of the establishment, and whose attire proclaimed them to be the possessors of great wealth (or, at any rate, of expensive wardrobes).

We leaned patiently against a gigantic marble column, while intimate glimpses of a great number of the guests were revealed to us, as well as hasty views of kitchens, swimming-pools, ball-rooms, elevators, dining-rooms, corridors, roof-gardens, and telephone switchboards, all constructed upon a scale which dwarfed anything that I had ever seen upon our own planet.

With these helpful but rather fatiguing preliminaries disposed of, we were permitted to ascend to the room to which we had been assigned. Like everything else in the hotel, its dimensions were colossal, and the furniture exceeded, both in size and in profusion, any that I had ever seen in a terrestrial hotel. The bathroom (which was by far the largest that I had ever seen) contained a magnificent sunken swimming bath as its sole furniture. I was more than a little surprised to find so luxurious a hotel lacking in those conveniences to which even the humblest humans are accustomed. But this lack of conveniences (as I discovered only too often to my embarrassment and discomfort) is universal in Purilia – a curious fact which I can attribute only to the physiological differences between the Purilians and ourselves, to which I have already made reference.

Johnson and I now debated ways and means of conducting our search for Pansy and Mollie. The task before us was a stupendous one. Where, among all these teeming millions, could one hope to find two obscure young girls from the country? We did not know how to begin. At length we determined to enlist the aid of the police and set out forthwith for the nearest police station.

As we opened the door of our room, and stepped into the corridor, I observed a uniformed bell-boy slinking stealthily up the staircase just opposite. But at the moment I attached no particular significance to this obviously suspicious conduct.

While we were waiting for the elevator, the Presence made one of those casual and unheralded announcements, to which we had by now become accustomed: 'Dorothy,' it said, 'reared in poverty, but with a love of all the fine things which only the fortunate rich can enjoy.' Turning, we saw a young and beautiful girl, dressed in the uniform of a chambermaid, approaching us. Her face wore a rather blank expression which, had I been more familiar with the peculiarities of Purilian physiognomy, would have conveyed to me that she was harbouring a mysterious and important secret.

As she passed us, she dropped at my feet, with obvious deliberation, a tiny wad of paper. Greatly astonished, I picked it up, and was about to ask the girl the meaning of her strange conduct, when the door of the elevator opened. Hastily motioning to us to enter the elevator, and then indicating the necessity of secrecy by putting her finger significantly to her lips, Dorothy hurried away down the corridor.

As the elevator descended, I opened the tightly folded bit of paper. It proved to be a note, written in a round girlish hand. It bore neither superscription nor signature and contained only the words: 'Be careful, you are being watched.'

The effect of this upon us can well be imagined. Here we were, two strangers in the great metropolis, engaged upon a search of almost unparalleled difficulty, and to add to our troubles we were being subjected to espionage. I understood now the suspicious conduct of the bell-boy. Undoubtedly, he had been listening outside of our door and was fully conversant with our plan to go to the police station. (Purilian servants, I discovered, are, on the whole, an untrustworthy lot. More often than not they are in the pay of the enemies of their employers. They spend much of their time in eavesdropping and peeping through keyholes, but fortunately they conduct these nefarious operations with great clumsiness and consequently are almost invariably detected.)

But who was having us watched and why? To these questions we could find no answer. Dorothy's conduct made clear that our danger was a grave one and that she herself was incurring a considerable risk in informing us of it. Obviously we were becoming more and more involved in the entanglements of Purilian life.

Our egress from the hotel was delayed by a little man, with enormous shoes and baggy trousers, several sizes too large for him, who had become entrapped in the revolving door, the nature of which he did not seem to understand. Around and around he went, like a squirrel in a cage, the door revolving, with ever-increasing rapidity. The poor fellow seemed quite unable to extricate himself until, at length, the whirling door catapulted him into the street. An involuntary somersault ended in his becoming tightly wedged in a perambulator, which happened to be passing just at that moment. The occupant of the perambulator, a lusty and well-developed child, fixed its teeth firmly in the little man's leg, and, to make matters worse, the mother of the child, a rather stout woman, belaboured the unhappy intruder with her umbrella.

I learned, subsequently, that this little man was a member of a numerous and rather important Purilian sub-caste. These little fellows – for they are all undersized and all recognizable by the sartorial oddities to which I have referred – are frequently encountered in all parts of Purilia. Despite their essential ingenuousness, it must be confessed that they make rather a nuisance of themselves, because of the fact that they are utterly incapable of adapting themselves to the mechanical contrivances of an industrial civilization. Whether this is due merely to a lack of co-ordination, or whether they are archaic survivals of a race of prehistoric Purilians, I am unable to say. But in either case they are a curious anomaly in a world which demands an ability to adjust oneself to complex mechanisms.

The incident of the revolving door is typical of the difficulties in which these little men constantly find themselves. Elevators, escalators, electric-fans, high-pressure fire-hose, and derricks are but a few of the devices which involve them in the most distressing misadventures. It is a miracle that any of them manages to survive. But, somehow or other, they always seem able to escape the consequences of their ineptitude, as well as to get the better of the police, whose relentless hostility they invariably incur. Their lives, however, as will be readily understood, are far from pleasant and when one considers, too, that their unprepossessing appearance makes them unworthy objects of spiritual love, it is not surprising that sad hearts lurk beneath their grotesque exteriors and that one cannot regard them without feeling a sense of the most profound pathos. Their hard lot, naturally enough, makes them rather antisocial and they often express their animosity by bombarding the objects of their displeasure with succulent pastry and other curious missiles, which they always seem to have at hand. On the whole, they could scarcely be regarded as assets to any civilization.

We made our way to the police station, through streets in which crime was rampant. Assaults, gunfire, and hand-to-hand struggles were commonplace incidents, and innumerable pursuits, on foot and in vehicles, wound their way diligently through the mazes of metropolitan traffic.

Our recourse to the police was worse than useless. When we succeeded in arousing the desk-sergeant, whom we found sound asleep, with his feet upon the desk, he listened to our story with complete indifference. We learned that Pansy and Mollie were only two of the thousands of rural girls who were lost in the great city, and that the chances of finding them through so conventional an agency as police investigation were practically negligible.

We left the station, greatly disheartened. But had we tarried for a moment to eavesdrop, we should have been greatly alarmed, too. For scarcely had we left the station before the sergeant made haste to telephone to Millwood all the details of our visit. But we did not learn of this until later, when we discovered that Millwood was not only in collusion with the police, but was a powerful force in the city's underworld, too.

As we made our way dejectedly back to the hotel, we came to the intersection of the city's two most important thoroughfares, and as we waited for an opportunity to make our way across, the Presence remarked: 'The crossroads of Purilia, where every man, woman, and child goes by at least once in his life.'

At once, Johnson and I were struck by the same thought. If we took up our station at this intersection, we should be certain eventually of seeing Pansy and Mollie go by. Here, at last, was a tangible hope! There were, of course, two possible objections: one, that we might have to maintain our vigil for months, or even years, before the girls went by; and the other, that perhaps they had gone by already. But since the plan was so much more constructive than any we had yet hit upon we determined to try it, and we agreed to alternate in maintaining a lookout for the girls, relieving each other every eight hours.

Johnson insisted upon having the first watch, and so I left him at the corner and returned to the hotel, considerably heartened by the hope that our vigil would be rewarded with success.

I entered our room, without catching another glimpse of

Dorothy, and, seating myself at the writing-desk, began to make some entries in my notebook, which until now I had sadly neglected. I filled a page rapidly and, taking up a large piece of blotting-paper, was about to apply it to the wet ink, when I noticed that there appeared upon it several lines of handwriting, left there no doubt by a previous occupant of the room. The script was, of course, in reverse and quite illegible; but overcome with curiosity I held up the blotter before a mirror, and was able to read the reflected writing with ease.

These were the words that revealed themselves to my astounded gaze: 'I rely upon you to see that they do not come out alive.' The handwriting was only too familiar. It was the same hand that had penned that fatal note to Pansy – Millwood's!

For a few moments I was dazed and confused; but slowly the situation became clear to me. Or, at any rate, what became clear was that Millwood had managed to precede us to the city, that he had occupied that very room the night before, and that he was determined, at any cost, to prevent Johnson and me from succeeding in our quest – for I had not the least doubt that the 'they,' in the letter referred to us.

I was convinced now that the bell-boy was one of Millwood's satellites whom he had set to spy upon us. Apparently, the man's villainous resourcefulness knew no bounds.

But to whom was the letter written? And by what means did Millwood propose to put us out of the way? And was he, too, still searching for the girls, or had they already fallen into his clutches? These questions, and a dozen more, it was impossible to answer. But it was enough to know that not only were the girls the intended victims of some diabolical scheme, but our own lives were grievously endangered. I determined to hurry back to Johnson at once, and acquaint him with these serious developments.

CHAPTER 10

BUT when I reached the street corner where I had left Johnson, I was astonished and disconcerted to find that he was not there. I made a slow and careful tour of the adjoining corners, scanning every face and even peering into doorways and shops, but there was no sign of Johnson. Then I returned to the appointed post and paced back and forth uneasily, on the chance that Johnson would appear presently. But after a half-hour or more of this fruitless waiting, I determined to return to the hotel, hoping to find there either Johnson or some message informing me of his whereabouts.

As I turned my steps toward the hotel, a rough-looking fellow, heavily bearded and with a cap pulled down over his eyes, brushed against me with what appeared to be such unpardonable rudeness that I was about to rebuke him sharply, when, to my amazement, he whispered in my ear: 'Johnson is on Mollie's trail. The Chinks have got hold of her.'

For a moment I was literally paralysed with astonishment and when I turned to question my informant he had already disappeared in the crowd. I did not even attempt to look for him, eager as I was to obtain an explanation of his utterance, for it was obvious, now, that his beard and lowered cap were a disguise, the removal of which would make identification impossible.

But the message, even without elucidation, conveyed clearly that Mollie was in some sort of danger, from which Johnson was trying to extricate her. Who the Chinks were and what was the nature of their menace, I had not the least notion; and, while I stood wondering how I could procure information on these points, an incident occurred which, for the moment, drove all thoughts of Mollie and of Johnson from my mind.

A pedestrian, hurrying by, happened to drop at my feet the illustrated supplement of a newspaper, which he was carrying under his arm. As I stooped mechanically to pick it up and return it to him, my eye was caught by a photograph of a group of girls in ballet dress, which appeared in a prominent place upon the front page of the supplement. Judge my astonishment when, in the very centre of the group, I recognized the lovely features of Pansy! I looked again, scarcely able to believe the evidence of my senses. But there was no doubt about it: it was Pansy beyond question.

Under the photograph, was an explanatory legend which read: 'The Bevy of Fast-Stepping Cuties who are packing 'em in every night at the Palais Royale Night-Club. Can they toddle? And how!' I deduced from this that Pansy had obtained employment as a dancer in a cabaret (a supposition which events proved to be correct). The reader can imagine my elation at this timely discovery. I determined to follow the valuable clue without a moment's delay – especially since no way of rendering immediate assistance to Johnson seemed to present itself.

The driver of a passing taxicab knew the address of the Palais Royale Night-Club, and I directed him to convey me there at once. It took but a few minutes to reach the night-club and, save for a rather brutal murder in a neighbouring taxicab, the journey was without incident. As my taxicab came to a halt in front of the brightly lighted resort, the Presence remarked: 'The Palais Royale, where wine, woman, and song reign supreme, and thoughtless gaiety takes a heavy toll of youth and beauty.' And, as I entered the ornate portals, it vouchsafed this further information: 'In the jazz symphony of life, there are many blue notes.'

The introduction was not a promising one, and I was not without misgivings for Pansy's welfare. At the entrance to the dining-room, I was met by a faultlessly tailored man with waxed moustache who, it developed, was the head waiter

(Henri by name). Although the place was crowded almost to suffocation, there happened to be a vacant table beside the cleared space reserved for the entertainment, and to this Henri courteously conducted me.

Just as I took my place, the ballet was making its bow in response to enthusiastic applause; but, before I had an opportunity to note whether or not Pansy was among them, the girls had disappeared again. I learned to my chagrin that it would be a half-hour, at least, before they made their next appearance. There was nothing to do but wait, and, having ordered some refreshment, I settled back in my chair with the intention of making such observations as time permitted.

The night-club, although by far the largest place of the kind I had ever seen, was, as I have said, uncomfortably crowded. The guests were all in a state of most demonstrative hilarity. There was much shouting and violent gesticulating and uproarious laughter, although there seemed to be very little reason for any of it. Many of the diners wore caps of coloured tissue-paper and seemed to derive much enjoyment from the grotesque effects produced by this headgear. Great streamers of coloured paper were flung about the room in every direction, and innumerable gas balloons, of enormous size, were tossed about gaily, from table to table. All this made it difficult to eat and drink with any degree of comfort; but this no one seemed to mind, and, in fact, except for an occasional fist-fight between two men over the affections of a woman, and the unpleasant attempts of a man, here and there, to force his attentions upon an unwilling girl, everyone behaved with extreme good humour. Music was supplied by a Negro orchestra, whose antics threw the guests into convulsions of mirth.

(The American reader will perhaps be interested in a brief account of the status of the Negro race in Purilia. Upon the happy absence of those devastating racial antagonisms with which we on earth are only too familiar, I have already

87

commented. There is, therefore, no Negro problem in Purilia. Throughout my entire sojourn in the country, I was struck by its complete freedom from all those thorny social questions which, among us, are always created by the presence of a Negro element in the population. Miscegenation is unknown; and the question of political and social equality has never even been raised. It is not so much that the Purilian Negro knows his place, as that his place is immutably fixed by the natural laws of the country.

(The Purilian Negroes are a happy, childlike race, given to song and laughter. Spiritual love, or in fact any kind of love, is totally foreign to their nature, and their lives are happily free from any form of tragedy or suffering. Indeed, their only personal problem, of any consequence, concerns itself with the evasion of disembodied spirits, of which they are in constant terror. This unwarranted and often rather ludicrous phobia is readily aroused by any object that even remotely suggests the supernatural. Cats, because of their peculiar habits of becoming entangled in sheets and pillow-cases, and of emerging unexpectedly from flour-bins, are particular objects of superstitious dread to the Purilian Negroes; and the mere sight of one of these transfigured felines will cause a member of the Negro race – all of whom are exceedingly fleet-footed – to run innumerable miles, without a backward glance, under the false impression that he is being pursued by a ghostly apparition. In the course of these flights, the Negroes often cause much damage to person and property. But aside from this rather extraordinary idiosyncrasy, the Negroes are, as I have said, a peaceable and happy race.

(Occupationally, the male Negroes are, almost without exception, either musicians or Pullman porters. The females, nearly all of whom are well past middle age, are, for the most part, superannuated nursemaids whose sole interest in life is the welfare of the white men and women whom they cared for in infancy, and for the sake of whose happiness they

88

would willingly lay down their own lives. The Purilian Negro has no thought of entering the arts or the professions, and in consequence there are in Purilia no Negro poets, lawyers, doctors, or teachers.

The diet of the Purilian Negro is a simple one, consisting almost entirely of chicken and water-melon. For some inexplicable reason, these delicacies are enjoyed most when obtained by stealth, and, in fact, an otherwise law-abiding Negro will stop at nothing to obtain the coveted viands. I am convinced that, if the Purilian Negro could be persuaded to adopt a more varied diet, another element in the country's all-pervading lawlessness would be eliminated. But, unfortunately, there is no machinery for the institution of social reforms, and even the most advanced Purilians are so absorbed in their own emotional problems that it is impossible to interest them in a broader social view.)

While I was making my observations of the night-club, the Presence remarked, 'Emily, one of the reasons for the popularity of the Palais Royale' – thereby calling my attention to a young and beautiful girl who was preparing to sing, to the accompaniment of a middle-aged female, hard-visaged and decidedly foreign-looking.

I watched Emily with great interest, until the swelling faces of two men at the next table diverted my attention to them. One of the men was stout and the other thin, but they both wore moustaches and smoked cigars, so I suspected that they were there for no good purpose. They were watching Emily attentively, and the thin man was rolling his cigar between his lips, in a way that I afterwards learned is always indicative of lust.

I now divided my attention between Emily and my neighbours. It was obvious from the girl's manner that she did not enjoy her work; in fact, she wore what seemed to me an expression of undisguised loathing. I could not help wondering what had made her choose a profession that was apparently so distasteful; but as none of her auditors, more particularly my two neighbours, appeared to notice anything singular in the girl's manner, I began to think that I must be mistaken.

Upon the conclusion of her song, there was vociferous applause, led by the lean man, who winked at his neighbour in a highly significant manner.

'You're wasting your time,' said his stout companion, shaking his head. 'Emily is different.'

The thin man laughed unpleasantly. 'Just watch me,' he said, ominously.

At this moment, Emily passed close to my neighbours' table. The lean man bent forward and, taking her hand, drew her toward him. The girl's face wore a look of repulsion such as I had never seen before, and I thought it remarkable that her admirer did not appear to notice it. The next moment, I was surprised to see him produce from his pocket a flat box which, when opened, revealed the largest diamond bracelet that had ever come under my notice. Still miling significantly, he snapped the bracelet on to the girl's' wrist and held it up for her admiration.

'For me?' said Emily, although it seemed evident that the man clearly intended it for her.

The man nodded. 'Yes, for you,' he said, removing her doubts.

At this moment, I became aware of a woman, no longer young, who was seated at a table near by, watching the scene with unconcealed interest. Indeed, she was glaring malevolently at Emily's admirer, her hands clenched and her bosom profoundly agitated. Her identity was soon revealed to me, by the Presence, who announced: 'Meg Davis had lived and loved – and lost.'

Emily now unfastened the bracelet from her wrist and, handing it back to the man, said: 'Thank you; but I couldn't dream of accepting it.' The man raised his eyebrows, in evident surprise, while his stout companion laughed audibly and poked him in the ribs. But the thin man was not abashed.

'No?' he said to Emily, with an unpleasant smile. 'Then I'll send it back and get a bigger one.'

I could see that he had mistaken the reason for Emily's refusal of the bracelet. The other guests, who had waited patiently during this interlude, now clamoured for a repetition of Emily's song. She excused herself hastily, and went back to the piano. Meg continued to glare at the man; and I was alarmed to see her open her purse and extract what appeared to be a small revolver. Her conduct filled me with foreboding.

As Emily prepared to sing, I heard her middle-aged accompanist whisper to her: 'Don't be foolish, little one; he's very rich.' But the splendid girl shook her head firmly, and said, with deep conviction, 'There can be no love without honour.' Having given utterance to this admirable sentiment, she repeated her song with tremendous effect; although, for me, its enjoyment was somewhat impaired by my consciousness of Meg's laboured breathing and my sense of impending tragedy. (How much more disturbed would I have been had I known that Millwood was watching me closely, from behind a pillar!)

Amid riotous enthusiasm, such as I have seldom seen equalled, Emily, for the second time, began to make her exit. Again, as she passed my neighbour's table, the lean man drew her toward him. 'How about a little supper after the show?' he said. 'My limousine is waiting.' As the harassed girl drew back, in disgust, I saw Meg's enlarged forefinger reach toward the electric-light switch which happened to be just behind her.

Instantly, the place was plunged into darkness. Then a shot was fired; and, when amid shrieks and shouts the lights were flashed on again, Emily's persecutor lay dead upon the floor. I had scarcely time to note that Meg had disappeared; for the scene of confusion which ensued engaged all my attention. Tables were upset and crockery broken, as men and women threshed about, in what seemed to me a rather aimless fashion. Then, as someone raised the cry of, 'The police, the police!' the panic became a stampede. Unable to resist the tide, I was swept along, out of the night-club and into the street, fully aware, even in my frantic struggle to maintain my footing, that I was perhaps losing my chance of a meeting with Pansy.

CHAPTER 11

ONCE in the street, I managed to extricate myself from the crowd and, bent upon finding Pansy, began to look for some means of re-entering the night-club. But my efforts were useless. Police officers had arrived in great numbers, and, despite my entreaties and explanations, I was ordered to move on.

As I walked reluctantly away, a young and handsome man stepped out of a doorway and intercepted me. I noted, not without surprise, that he wore a checked cap and a coarse flannel shirt, which contrasted strangely with his well-tailored clothes. Before the youth had time to address me, the Presence, whose helpful assistance I was beginning to regard as almost indispensable, remarked: 'Jack Vanderbrook, heir to his father's millions, but unspoiled by great wealth.'

I looked, with renewed interest, at the young millionaire, who now began to question me eagerly concerning the events at the night-club. It seemed that he had long been enamoured of the young singer Emily, but, fearing that knowledge of his wealth might influence her to grant him an affection which she otherwise would have withheld, he determined to conceal from her his true economic position. As he himself put it, 'I wanted her to love me for myself alone.'

Accordingly, he had hit upon the ingenious device of wearing a cap and a flannel shirt whenever he had occasion to meet Emily, thereby giving her the impression that he was poor. But the splendid girl had met the test admirably. Although believing Jack to be penniless, she had freely expressed her reciprocation of his love; and the happy fellow had intended that very evening to ask Emily's hand in marriage.

But only a few hours before, while he had been making his way, on foot, to the night-club, he was horrified to see Emily in a limousine, in company with a well-known club-man named Garrison (who, I gathered from his description, was the man I had just seen murdered). Naturally, this had made Jack assume that Emily had been playing him false and that there existed an illicit relationship between her and Garrison. His joyous expectancy had given way to bitter disillusionment and despair, and for hours, he had paced the streets in the vicinity of the night-club, not knowing what course to pursue. The hasty emptying of the night-club and the arrival of the police had made him suspect that something was wrong and, in consequence, he was greatly concerned about the safety of Emily, whom, I inferred, he still loved passionately.

I told him briefly what had occurred. He listened, with intense interest, and when I described Garrison's death he exclaimed, with flashing eyes and clenched teeth: 'He deserved what he got. He was a lizard who preyed on decent women.'

He then questioned me closely concerning the identity of Garrison's slayer. I explained that the fatal shot had been fired in the dark, but that I suspected Meg. To my surprise, Vanderbrook scouted this hypothesis, and I gathered that he believed that Emily was the guilty person, his hypothesis being that Garrison had betrayed the girl (although in what way he did not make clear) and that she had avenged herself by putting an end to the fellow's existence. Convinced of the girl's guilt, Jack determined now to save her from the consequences of her act. 'It's no crime,' he said heatedly, 'to kill a rat like that.' Of course, marriage between him and Emily was now out of the question, but the tradition of his class made it imperative for him to rescue the girl from her predicament. He told me that he was prepared, if necessary, even to take the crime upon himself. This I thought a little quixotic, but the Presence, as though to remove my doubts, remarked explanatorily: 'Chivalry has ever been the instinctive gesture of a gentleman.'

Vanderbrook now informed me of his intention of going to the studio of an artist of his acquaintance, who had arranged a small midnight party for some of the night-club's performers. There he hoped to find Emily. I now explained, eagerly, my quest for Pansy and asked if he thought it probable that she would be present at the party, too. He assured me that it was more than likely, and graciously asked me to accompany him.

I gladly accepted his invitation and we hurried to Jack's home in order that he might assume more appropriate garments. He was kind enough, too, to offer to supply me with correct attire.

I now had my first glimpse of the domestic life of the Purilian plutocracy. The Vanderbrook home was a magnificent mansion, almost equal in size to the Metropolis Hotel. The rooms were built upon a scale which dwarfed the occupants. Innumerable servants were posted stiffly about or moved noiselessly, here and there, on mysterious errands. Numerous animals were visible, too. In addition to dogs of various breeds and pedigreed cats, there were monkeys, parrots, and ornate cages housing little song-birds. Aquatic life was represented by several large aquariums and a sunken tank, in which an alligator dozed. The staircases were superb, being easily wide enough to have admitted the passage of two motor-buses; the lofty corridors faded away in the distance; and Jack's room, to which several servants escorted us, was reminiscent of one of our metropolitan railway terminals.

But, lest the reader be moved to envy by my description of this splendour, let me hasten to assure him that in Purilia the lot of the rich is a most unhappy one. That money cannot buy happiness is a truism which one finds amply illustrated throughout the land. Happiness comes only through love, and in the vast, chill halls which the Purilian rich inhabit that tender plant does not thrive.

Indeed, no worse misfortune can befall one in Purilia than to be born of wealthy parents. Mother-love, the greatest of Purilian institutions, can scarcely be said to exist among the wealthy. Almost invariably, the unlucky infant millionaire is completely neglected, or even despised, by its mother, who occupies herself solely with self-adornment and the pursuit of selfish pleasures (in which, however, she never succeeds in finding happiness). These children, although provided with every luxury, are usually undersized and rather anaemic and, soon tiring of their expensive toys, spend almost all their time pining for the maternal love of which they have been robbed, and envying the happy little street-gamins, for whom a pair of loving arms is always waiting.

Nor can their lot be said to be improved, when they attain marriageable age; for, among the wealthy, parental opposition to the marriages which their offspring desire is almost universal. Or, if the parents are no longer living, they have imposed so many conditions in their wills as to make a free choice almost impossible. In fact, these testamentary eccentricities of the Purilian upper classes are a constant source of unhappiness and add another troublesome element to the complications of Purilian life.

The whole business of the disposition of the property of deceased persons is sadly in need of reform. Quite apart from the troublesome documents to which I have referred, the utmost carelessness is evident with regard to wills. Last testaments are frequently stolen, lost, or mislaid; or, worse still, persons who should know better allow themselves to be taken in by the crudest forgeries. All this has a most unsettling effect upon the economic life of the country – to say nothing of the personal fortunes of the individuals concerned. Fortunately, though, in the end, justice almost always triumphs.

The better sort among the young millionaires – of whom Jack Vanderbrook was one – always seek to negative the curse of wealth by choosing as mates Pudencians of humble origin. These girls usually decline at first the millionaires' offers of marriage, either because they fear that they will handicap their wealthy lovers, or because they prefer their simple homes to the splendid foyers of the rich; but love eventually conquers their objections.

With the assistance of two or three valets, Jack and I dressed for the party and, suitably attired, prepared to depart. We left Jack's suite and walked along the corridor to the distant stairway; but we had proceeded only a few hundred yards when the house was filled with a frightful commotion. Shots, the sound of breaking glass, and the screams of women rent the air.

We rushed downstairs and found that the servants had just frustrated the attempts of a band of burglars to make off with the crown-jewels of a former empress, which Jack's mother had purchased only that morning. To my dismay I saw among the captured thieves the hotel chambermaid Dorothy, who had put me on my guard against Millwood. The poor girl was in tears, but before I could attempt to comfort her the police arrived in large numbers. Jack's mother, a tall stern-faced woman in a luxurious negligée (the customary attire of Purilian women of wealth), harshly demanded that the officers apprehend the thieves and remove them, at once, to prison.

Almost as she spoke, cries of mutual recognition were uttered by Dorothy and one of the officers, a tall, handsome young fellow. 'Jerry!' cried Dorothy. 'Dorothy!' cried Jerry almost simultaneously. Then Dorothy hung her head in shame, while Jerry, stepping forward, said with deep conviction, 'I won't believe that the sweetest girl in the world is a crook.' But Dorothy was incapable of deceiving her trusting lover. 'It's all true, Jerry,' she said. 'I'm guilty, but I don't want you to think I'm a bad girl.' And sobbing, she flung herself into the young policeman's arms. Jerry shook his head sorrowfully. 'What made you do it?' he said. The girl looked up at him, her eyes dimmed with tears. 'I don't know,' she said, staring into space. 'I think I must have gone mad.'

She now went on to explain how she had become involved in this lamentable situation. Robbed in infancy of a mother's love, and subjected to the maltreatment of a stern father, she had always longed for those luxuries which only the very rich can afford. This love for beautiful things had led her into the company of a band of criminals who, taking advantage of her youthful innocence, had used her as a tool in the furtherance of their nefarious schemes. It was she who had informed the thieves of the transfer of the crown-jewels to Mrs Vanderbrook, by a foreign jeweller who was a guest at the Metropolis Hotel. And she had accompanied the burglars upon their expedition to the Vanderbrook home without clearly realizing what she was doing.

It was evident from the girl's story that, although technically guilty, she was really morally innocent; and Jack and I sought to prevail upon Mrs Vanderbrook to let the girl go. But the woman harshly refused, and poor Dorothy seemed doomed. Suddenly, however, Jack, as though by inspiration, reminded his mother of the fact that Dorothy bore the same name as his younger sister, who had died in infancy, partly as a result of maternal neglect. Conscience-stricken, Mrs Vanderbrook melted and, taking Dorothy in her arms, offered to adopt her as her own daughter, to fill the place in her heart left vacant by the death of the little one, years before. This offer was gratefully accepted by Dorothy; and, indeed, it was a pleasant alternative to the long prison-sentence with which she had been faced only a moment before.

The beaming Jerry now opened his arms to her again, and, as the happy girl nestled against his shoulder, he said, with a flash of native wit: 'It's a life sentence you'll get now!'

The other prisoners were hurried off to their just punishment; and Jack and I left for the party. As I passed Dorothy, she slipped into my hand a folded bit of paper. I did not open it until we were seated in Jack's limousine, when I glanced at it hastily. It contained only the words: 'Be careful, Millwood means trouble.'

And, as the limousine rolled away from the kerb, I saw, crouched in the shadows, a yellow-faced, slant-eyed figure.

CHAPTER 12

When we arrived at the artist's studio, we found it already crowded with guests. The studio was most spacious, and its luxurious furnishings were ample proof that the practice of the plastic arts in Purilia brings with it a greater financial reward than is the case upon our planet. This I found puzzling, for nowhere had I seen any evidence of a taste for the fine arts.

(This impression was confirmed by later observations. Not once did I encounter any Purilian in whose life either aesthetic experience or critical appreciation of the arts played the slightest part. The enjoyment of literature, too, is a comparatively unknown pleasure. Young men and young women are sometimes seen to pick up a book, but they do so always with the hope that perusal of the volume will help them forget some deep sorrow. Reading for pleasure is confined almost entirely to fathers of a superior type. These kindly, dignified elderly men, pipe in mouth and clad in dressing-gown and slippers, occasionally settle down to a good book, from the enjoyment of which they are snatched, all too often, by the necessity of helping to solve some particularly knotty emotional problem in the lives of their offspring.)

Jack had assured me that our host was something of a genius, and I looked about eagerly in the hope of finding some examples of his work. I was rather disappointed to find the studio ornamented with works of decidedly inferior quality. There were paintings and sculptures in abundance – all of extraordinary size – but, despite my own meagre acquaintance with the arts, I was rather shocked by the conspicuously bad taste which characterized these objects. One curious fact about the works displayed was that, while none of them could exactly be said to represent the nude female figure, they all somehow suggested it. And, indeed, I discovered later that, to the Purilian, nudity and plastic art are almost interchangeable concepts.

I tried to discover to what school our host belonged and what were his stylistic peculiarities. But no one seemed to know or, indeed, to apprehend the nature of my inquiry. I was even more astonished to discover that no one could inform me whether he was a sculptor or a painter, or seemed even to be aware that there is any difference between the two. The term 'artist', I learned, referred rather to a mode of living than to the practice of an art, the word being eulogistic in connotation when applied to a dead person, and somewhat opprobrious when applied to a living one.

And, indeed, the Purilian artist is far from an admirable person. He is either a rather ridiculous, down-at-heels fellow, untidy in person and given to eccentricities in dress, and displaying often many of the symptoms of insanity; or else (as was the case with our host) he is a dissolute debauchee, who spends his substance in riotous living and with whom no woman is safe (although here, again, I am unable to say in just what way her safety is menaced).

Our host, whose face bore clearly the marks of dissipation, greeted us in the foyer and, as he led us toward the huge room filled with guests, I was a little surprised to hear Jack say, with apparent friendliness: 'It looks like a good party. I don't think we'll regret that we came.' The host, however,

99

far from taking offence, seemed, to my surprise, to regard this remark as complimentary.

The room was gay, with long streamers of coloured paper and with large gas balloons, which the guests tossed merrily about. Many of the guests, too, wore caps of coloured tissue-paper and some, I noted with interest, wore masquerade-dress and dominoes. Everyone was hilarious, almost to the point of boisterousness, although there seemed little occasion for it. A Negro orchestra, larger than any I had ever before seen in a private home, supplied the music and most of the guests were dancing animatedly, but with a self-consciousness that I thought rather odd in sophisticated adults.

Suddenly, a girl jumped upon a table and, mounting thence upon the shoulders of two men, requested silence in order that she might sing. There was much vociferous applause, and the girl, leaping lightly to the ground, took her place beside an enormous concert piano, where an emaciated man with a luxuriant growth of hair now seated himself. (This man, I learned, was an eminent composer; but, beyond that, I could discover nothing concerning him.)

The gaiety of the guests now gave place to grave attentiveness, as the girl began to sing; and, as it soon became evident that the song was of a serious character, the faces of the listeners began to reflect thoughtful sobriety. The song was a rather simple ballad, concerning itself with an elderly Negro, named Joe, who, upon his death-bed, experienced the hallucination of being summoned by a choir of angels to a happy life in the world beyond the grave. The effect of this song upon the listeners was rather startling. Never before had I seen men and women so deeply moved by music. Everywhere, I saw trembling lips and lowered eyelids; and, when the young singer tremulously uttered the familiar name of the moribund black, by which, he fancied, the angelic chorus called him, many of the women sobbed aloud and more than one man hastily dashed an unwonted tear from his eye. The song finished, the singer received a tremendous ovation; and I was gratified to see that the director of an opera company, who was among the guests, offered her immediately a long engagement upon the most flattering terms.

Naturally, I had scanned the faces of the guests eagerly, in the hope of finding Pansy; but she was nowhere to be seen. Suddenly, however, Jack gripped my arm and drew me quickly to a little group surrounding Emily, who was describing the happenings which had preceded the tragic incident at the night-club. We quietly joined the group, Jack standing with averted face, so that Emily would not recognize him (although, as she had seen him only in his cap and flannel shirt, it is improbable that she would have known him, in any case, in his evening-clothes).

Emily now told, tearfully, of her love for the handsome young pauper – which, of course, she supposed Jack to be – and of her grief at not finding him at his accustomed post when she left the night-club. She expressed the fear that her lover might mistakenly have received the impression that she had been interested in Garrison. She voiced her hatred of Garrison in unqualified terms, but explained how, that afternoon, seeking to escape the unwelcome attentions of another man, she had impulsively stepped into a limousine which was standing at the curb, quite unaware that the vehicle was Garrison's. A moment later, Garrison had entered the limousine and, mistaking the reason for her presence there, had ordered the chauffeur to drive off, before Emily was able to escape. A cry of joy now sprang from Jack, at this convincing proof of Emily's innocence – not only of the murder of Garrison, but of a betrayal of her lover as well.

He shouldered his way through the group about Emily, and, taking the startled girl in his arms, said: 'Forgive me, darling. I wronged you more than I can tell you.' So astonished was Emily that she had the utmost difficulty in recognizing him. 'Why, Jack,' she exclaimed, 'is it really you?' Convinced, at length, that it was, she listened in amazement, while Jack revealed his identity and apologized for the innocent deception which he had practised upon her. 'I just wanted to test you,' he said, 'but you stood the test well.' The happiness of the delighted girl was protractedly apparent. Jack now took a flat box from his pocket, and, opening it, revealed a necklace of magnificent pearls. As he placed the pearls about the girl's neck, he said: 'These were my mother's pearls. She told me she wanted them to be my wife's.' Emily fingered the pearls in bewilderment. 'For me?' she said, incredulously, unable to believe that the pearls were really hers.

Our host, learning now of this happy reunion, sprang upon a table and proposed a toast to the happy pair. After a few felicitous words (which were rewarded with riotous applause) he called for a glass in which to drink to the young couple. But before one could be procured, a merry girl swung her leg high and kicked off her slipper, which the artist caught laughingly and filled with champagne. The toast drunk, our genial host addressed his guests as follows: 'Life is short and we live but once. Let us eat, drink and be merry.'

These sentiments were greeted vociferously, and the guests immediately proceeded to act upon their host's advice. A girl sprang upon the table, and executed a dance of a highly erotic character. Persons who until now had given no evidence of intoxication suddenly began to reel and stagger, in a most alarming manner. Women flung themselves with abandon into men's arms. Lovely Pudencians repulsed with horror the advances of grey-haired Vauriens. More and more balloons were set afloat, and there was scarcely a head that did not bear a paper cap.

A little wearied by the hubbub and concerned, not only for Pansy, but for Johnson and Mollie, I retired to a chair near the door, with the intention of devising some plan of action. As I sat there, apart from the crowd, absorbed in my thoughts, I happened to attract the attention of a rather tipsy young woman, who suddenly and unexpectedly came over to me and perched herself upon my lap, her arms entwined about my neck. At almost the same instant, Pansy appeared in the doorway, and as she stood there for a moment her gaze fell full upon me. For some seconds she looked at me with a magnified expression, in which grief and contempt were mingled, and then, without a word, she turned and fled.

With the utmost difficulty, I extricated myself from the embrace of the intoxicated young woman, and hurried after Pansy. As I reached the pavement, she was just stepping into a taxicab, and before I could reach the kerb the vehicle drew away. Hastily hailing another taxicab, I directed the driver to follow Pansy's.

A long chase now ensued, through the mazes of metropolitan traffic. It seemed to me that we must have driven miles and miles. The crowded streets gave way to less populous thoroughfares, and soon we were racing through a suburban district, at a most perilous rate of speed. Then, somehow or other, we seemed to return to the city again and, before long, were once more proceeding through dense traffic. At one time we demolished an apple-cart, and at another we raced across some railroad-tracks, just in time to avoid annihilation by a speeding express-train.

But, just when it seemed that we were about to overtake Pansy, the passage of some fire-engines compelled us to halt, and, when we were able to proceed again, we had lost our quarry! I was almost beside myself with despair when, happening to glance at the floor of the taxicab, I observed a small white card. Picking it up mechanically, I was astonished and delighted to find that it was one of Pansy's visiting-cards, containing her address. It seems that the taxicab in which I was riding was the one which had conveyed Pansy to the party, and that in the course of her journey, no doubt, she had accidentally dropped one of her visiting cards. Heartened by this opportune discovery, I ordered the driver to proceed, at once, to the address indicated upon the card.

As we drove off, I observed that there was another taxi-cab behind us, but it did not occur to me, at the time, that I was being followed. We arrived presently at an apartment-house, and, dismissing the taxicab, I hurried into the building, ascertained the location of Pansy's apartment, and proceeded upstairs.

Pansy, herself, responded to my ring, and I could see that she had been weeping. At first she did not wish to permit me to enter, but finally I prevailed upon her and reluctantly she ushered me into her tiny sitting-room, the chief ornament of which was a large photograph of her missing brother.

But I had scarcely begun my explanation, when the door-bell rang again. As always, this threw Pansy into a state of painful consternation, and, almost hysterically, she pushed me into her bedroom (which adjoined the sitting-room) and closed the door behind me.

The door-bell rang again, but before Pansy had time to answer the summons the door burst violently open under the impact of a powerful shoulder. (I should explain that it is quite customary, in Purilia, for a man to effect his entrance into a room by lunging against the door and forcing it from its hinges.) From my hiding place I heard an all too familiar voice and, peeping through the keyhole, I saw that the intruder was Millwood. Two police officers accompanied him.

Pansy, her face expressing angry loathing, extended her arm and pointing to the door said, 'Leave my room at once, Mr Millwood.' But far from complying, Millwood laughed mockingly, and said with an unpleasant leer, 'I've come to take you home, my darling.' Pansy stared at him, her eyes wide with bewilderment. Then she said: 'What do you mean? I don't understand.' Millwood laughed. 'Have you forgotten,' he said, 'that we are married?' My amazement at hearing these words was exceeded only by Pansy's.

Clutching her agitated bosom, she staggered back a pace or two and cried: 'It's a lie, it's a lie!' One of the officers now stepped forward, and touching Millwood's shoulder said respectfully, 'Are you sure the lady is your wife, sir?'

Millwood smiled confidently and, taking a ring from his pocket, showed it to the officer. I recognized the ring, instantly, as Mrs Malone's wedding-ring, which Pansy had given as a pledge to the lawyer Billings. 'Look,' said Millwood to the police officer, showing him the inscription in the ring. ' "P. M. to H. M.," Pansy Malone to Horace Millwood. It's the ring she gave me, when we were wed.'

I was stunned by this evidence of Millwood's diabolical ingenuity. The reader need scarcely be told that the initials in the ring signified: 'Peter Malone to Helen Malone,' those being the names of Pansy's parents. But Millwood, with the connivance of Billings, had altered the meaning of the initials to serve his own purpose.

Pansy, of course, vehemently denied her marriage to Millwood, but without avail. To the police officers, the wedding-ring was convincing proof that Millwood and Pansy were man and wife. I was about to leave my hiding place and intervene, when Millwood caught sight of my hat, which was lying in a prominent place upon the table of the sitting-room. Pointing accusingly to the hat, he seized Pansy by the wrist and said between his clenched teeth: 'Well, what have you to say, now?'

Unwilling to remain longer in concealment, I now opened the door and stepped into the sitting-room. At the sound of my entrance, Millwood turned sharply and, pointing his forefinger at me, demanded, 'What were you doing in my wife's bedroom?' And before I could reply, he turned to the police officers and said: 'Arrest that man!'

The officers stepped forward and seized my arm. I asked one of them upon what charge I was being arrested and he replied with laconic grimness: 'You're wanted for the murder of "Bulldog" Garrison.'

The unexpectedness of this charge left me speechless. Pansy, forgetting her own predicament, rushed forward, and clutching the arm of one of my custodians exclaimed hysterically: 'Oh no, no, no, he didn't do it; he didn't do it!'

But the officers were deaf to her protests, as well as to those which I now uttered. For it seems that Millwood, who had been concealed behind a pillar at the night-club, had seen me there and had falsely reported to the police that I had fired the fatal shot. To make matters worse, one of the officers had been posted at the door of the night-club after the murder and had remembered my insistent attempts to re-enter the place, which had struck him, at the time, as highly suspicious. These facts, together with my unfortunate concealment in Pansy's bedroom, constituted a convincing case against me, and I gathered from the words and actions, not only of my custodians and accuser, but of Pansy as well, that my conviction was a foregone conclusion.

Still protesting my innocence, I was dragged off to prison, my concern for my own safety more than equalled by my fears for Pansy, left helpless now in Millwood's hands.

CHAPTER 13

THE next weeks were harrowing ones, indeed. Immediately after my arrest, I was indicted for the murder of Garrison; and then speedily tried, convicted, and sentenced to death by electrocution. I am confident that, judged dispassionately, the case against me was weak; and I do not believe that any human jury would have accepted the evidence which was presented as proof that I was guilty beyond that reasonable doubt, the benefit of which our Anglo-American jurisprudence allows the accused.

But Purilian juries are easily swayed; and a grave tactical error of my own contributed in large measure to my conviction. This occurred in the course of my defence, when, hoping to combat the evidence presented against me, I described the highly suspicious conduct of Meg Davis. But, far from aiding me, this ill-advised step prejudiced both judge and jury against me; for, in suggesting that Meg might have been the guilty person, I violated one of the cardinal principles of Purilian ethics, which prescribes that no man, no matter what the circumstances, must ever, by word or by deed, in any way compromise, endanger, or even inconvenience a woman. So that my mere mention of Meg served to convince everyone that I was a man without honour or principles, and hence it could be considered a certainty that I had murdered Garrison.

In vain, I pointed out that since I had never met Meg, it could scarcely be contended that I had any moral responsibility with regard to her, and that it would have been an act of quixotic folly, upon my part, willingly to have sacrificed my life to protect a person whom I did not even know. These arguments merely served to intensify the prejudice against me; indeed, the prevailing attitude can best be summarized in the words of the presiding judge, who said sternly: 'No gentleman, worthy of the name, could ever accuse a lady.'

I was handicapped, too, by my unfamiliarity with the legal procedure of Purilia, which differs considerably from ours – trials being conducted not so much for the purpose of arriving at a verdict (which is usually predetermined) as for affording an opportunity to the persons involved to make an effective display of their emotions. The rules of evidence are most elastic, and anyone so inclined is free to make extemporaneous statements or impassioned addresses to judge or jury. In addition, the trial is frequently halted in order to permit one or another of the principals to indulge in touching and intimate embraces with mother, spouse, sweetheart, or child. (Nevertheless, the judges are usually characterized by extreme harshness. They are armed with enormous gavels, with which they pound incessantly – without, however, having the slightest effect upon the spectators who weep, laugh, and applaud unrestrainedly.)

Despite the obvious prejudice against me, I heard the verdict of conviction rendered, and sentence pronounced upon me, with the utmost incredulity. Conscious as I was of my complete innocence, I was unable to believe that I had been actually condemned to death. In fact, it was not until I was led through the prison gates and heard the Presence announce, 'The grim Inferno whose frowning walls house the legion of the living dead,' that I fully realized what lay in store for me.

I was conveyed at once to a cell in the death-house – a huge edifice, crowded to overflowing with condemned men awaiting execution – and there I was left, to brood upon my fate. My sensations now were quite unlike those I had experienced during those hours in interstellar space, when it had seemed as though we might not reach Purilia and I had so clearly envisaged death. Then, while wishing yet to live, I knew that, if death came, it would be speedy and unavoidable, and a quite predictable consequence of our rash undertaking, for which we had only ourselves to blame. But now I was caught in the meshes of a legal and ethical system which I did not understand, and condemned to death for a crime of which I was wholly innocent. This palpable injustice engendered in me a bitter resentment, and for a few days I gave way to unrestrained rage against my fate and all those concerned in it.

But human emotion, unlike Purilian, soon spends itself; and before long I had begun to take account of my surroundings, and to attempt to devise some means of escaping my doom. Engaging my guards and my fellow prisoners in conversation, I soon made a discovery which not only filled me with astonishment, but tended to lessen my resentment of the injustice of which I was a victim. What I learned was the astonishing fact that practically every inmate of the death-house was innocent of the murder of which he had been convicted!

Further investigation revealed that, without exception, the condemned men had been convicted upon the flimsiest evidence conceivable. In some cases, the mere uncorroborated testimony of some designing person had been sufficient to bring about a conviction; in others, the accidental presence of the accused upon the scene of the crime had sufficed; in yet others, the weapon with which the crime had been committed had been found upon the person of the innocent defendant, placed there he knew not how. Many of the condemned, too, had voluntarily confessed guilt, in order to protect the good name of a woman; and others, for the same reason, had refused to defend themselves, although knowing well the identity of the guilty person.

So stunned was I by this revelation of a social system which permitted the finest flower of its youth – for the condemned were, almost to a man, young and handsome and possessed of high moral character – to be wantonly and unjustly deprived of life, that for a time I almost forgot the danger to which I myself was exposed. I was aware of the appalling frequency of murder in Purilia, and I could well understand that it was necessary to put into effect sternly repressive measures; but it seemed to me that there was little excuse for a system by whose operation the guilty always escaped and the innocent were always condemned.

My conclusion was hasty and premature; for, as day after day went by, I noted with amazement that no execution ever took place. As the last hour of each unhappy youth drew near, something fortunately intervened to prevent fulfilment of the sentence and to restore the convicted man to his loved ones, completely vindicated. A further inquiry revealed the startling fact that, although the death-house was always crowded with innocent men, there was no record of any of them having been executed!

I now saw the Purilian legal system in an entirely new

light. Conviction, I now understood, was proof, not of guilt, but of innocence; and once condemned to die a man could count upon his ultimate liberation with absolute certainty. So that the system, despite its apparent horrors, is actually a much more just and effective one than any we have been able to devise; for as a result of it the innocent always escape and the guilty are always punished.

Naturally, this discovery completely allayed my fears concerning my own fate, and I awaited the day set for my execution with equanimity, confident that something would happen to deliver me from death. Reassured as to my safety, I now sought to convince my fellow prisoners that, since there was no record of the execution of an innocent man, none of them had anything to fear. But, far from accepting the logic of my contention, they took my arguments in rather ill part, apparently resenting my suggestion that they had every reason to hope and none to despair. Sensible, now, of the danger of attempting to impose human logic upon the Purilians, I desisted from my attempts to cheer my fellow prisoners, and awaited impatiently the day appointed for my own execution.

I say impatiently, for not only was I confident now of my eventual liberation, but I was growing more concerned daily about the fate of both Johnson and Pansy. Furthermore, I began to find prison life most exhausting. The audible despair of my fellow prisoners and the religious exercises in which they were constantly engaged made rest almost impossible. The only time I could snatch a little sleep was during those moments in which the prisoners were occupied in fondling and feeding the little birds that hopped each day between the bars of the windows and whose visits alone brightened the dark hours of the unhappy Paragonian convicts.

Then, too, there was scarcely a day upon which some prisoner did not receive a visit from his mother or sweetheart – but I shall spare the reader an account of the agonizing scenes which ensued. At length, one day, I too had a visitor! The guard informed me that a lady had come to see me, and before I had recovered from my surprise a heavily veiled figure in black tottered to the bars of my cell, grasped my hands in hers, and then, without a word, tottered away again, sobbing violently. It was Pansy, of course, and, although I could have wished for an opportunity to learn what had befallen her, I was deeply grateful for the fleeting glimpse of her which had been afforded me.

The days dragged by, endlessly, but in due course my hour approached, and, although I had seen innumerable men snatched from death at the very last moment, I must confess that as my own time drew nearer my misgivings returned. At length only twelve hours remained and, although I still expected, at any moment, to receive favourable news, the guards assured me that I was hoping against hope, and that nothing could now intervene to save me. And, as hour succeeded hour, it seemed, indeed, as though they were right, and once more I contemplated death, made all the more bitter by the defeat of my confident hopes.

The appointed hour now arrived, and, accompanied by a minister of the Gospel, I was led to the lethal chamber amid the cheery farewells of my prison-mates. I recoiled at sight of the electric chair, but at the same instant my attentive ear caught the roaring of an aeroplane motor, which grew louder and louder, as I was placed in the instrument of death. As the straps were applied to my wrists and ankles, I could hear the plane circling overhead, and in another instant I knew that it had come to rest in the prison-yard. But, as I saw the warden raise his hand to give the fatal signal to the executioner, I entertained the grim conviction that, if relief for me had indeed come, it would be just a moment too late. At the very instant, however, that the executioner's hand tightened its grasp upon the annihilating lever, a guard burst into the chamber, crying 'Stop, stop!' And, as the warden turned to him in astonishment, the man breathlessly informed him that I was wanted in the prison office. The summons had come none too soon!

I was released from my bonds and, accompanied by the warden, proceeded, now, to the latter's office, where we found awaiting us Meg Davis, the district attorney, and a dignified, grey-haired man who I soon learned was the governor.

It seems that Meg, being (as I had suspected) guilty of Garrison's murder, had watched the approach of the day set for my execution with growing concern. For, although she was a murderess (and – worse yet – a woman whose life had not been all that it should have been) she was not without her better side, and she could not face calmly the prospect of an innocent man being done to death. Accordingly, she had informed the district attorney, just a few hours before my appointed time, that she had an important communication to make to him. The latter, eager to prevent the commission of irreparable injustice, had hastily enlisted the aid of the governor; and, the time being perilously short, they had chartered an aeroplane and had sped to the prison, arriving, as I have already related, not a moment too soon.

Meg now described the shooting of Garrison, freely admitting her guilt. 'He won my love,' she said, 'and then, when he grew tired of me, he flung me aside like a worn glove. That's why I made up my mind to put him where he never could harm anyone else.' Then, her eyes flashing and her head thrown back, she said, spiritedly: 'I'm glad I did it; he was a vile beast.'

It was evident that the district attorney and the governor were deeply impressed by the girl's story. I saw them exchange a significant look, and then, as though in response to a slow nod from the governor, the district attorney turned to the girl and said: 'I guess you've suffered enough. You'd better take a train to the country, where there are birds and mountains and trees.' Tears of gratitude filled the eyes of the bewildered girl. 'Do you really mean it?' she said. The district attorney assured her that he did, and, with lowered head, the girl walked slowly out of the warden's office.

The governor now turned to me and, putting his hand upon my shoulder, said: 'My boy, your sacrifice has not been in vain. Capital punishment will be abolished.' I was deeply gratified to learn that my incarceration had resulted in bringing about this important reform in the Purilian penal system, and I thanked the governor heartily.

The governor now pleaded an important engagement, at the executive mansion, and, as he opened his watch to apprise himself of the hour, I was amazed to see that the case contained a photograph which I recognized as that of Mrs Malone. An inquiry soon elicited the fact that he had been a youthful admirer of Mrs Malone and had hoped to marry her. But another had won her, and, although the wound had long since healed, he had never married and had always carried Mrs Malone's portrait in his watch, as a constant reminder of his unrequited love.

Upon making this discovery, I acquainted him with the misfortunes which had befallen Pansy. He expressed the deepest concern and offered to use his power in rescuing her from her difficulties. He agreed, at once, to pay Millwood the arrears of rent, thereby assuring the Malones' continued tenancy of the cottage and defeating Millwood's scheme to secure the rich oil deposits.

This necessary business disposed of, he promised to assist me in finding Pansy and disproving her marriage to Millwood. At this moment, one of the guards, who was a life-prisoner and a 'trusty', and who had been listening attentively to my conversation with the governor, stepped forward and informed us that he had just learned by the secret underground means of communication familiar to all criminals that Millwood, finding Pansy recalcitrant, had turned her over to the Chinks.

This alarming news spurred us to immediate action and, as soon as I had doffed my prison attire, we departed, bent upon succouring Pansy and hopeful, too, of finding Johnson and Mollie – the governor dismissing, in his anxiety for Pansy, the important affairs of state which awaited his attention.

CHAPTER 14

DURING my imprisonment I had made persistent inquiries concerning the Chinks, and as a result had gathered much detailed information about this strange and sinister race. The Chinks, it seems, having proved themselves altogether unassimilable to the prevailing industrial civilization of the whites, had established and maintained, in the very midst of this civilization, a social system entirely their own.

They are, to begin with, a burrowing people, who shun the light of day and habitually live subterranean lives. With infinite labour, they have constructed beneath the foundations of the city a metropolis of their own, in which they carry on their evil practices and weave their intricate plots for the undoing of guileless whites.

While the existence of this underground city is a matter of common knowledge, few whites have ever set foot in it, and even fewer have returned to tell the tale. For with almost superhuman ingenuity, the Chinks have succeeded in concealing so effectually every means of access to their city that even the shrewdest and most determined white finds it almost impossible to discover one of the gateways. Nor would the mere discovery of an entrance be of much assistance in penetrating the stronghold; for the invader would merely find himself in a labyrinth of dark and winding passageways. Here he might wander helplessly for hours or even for days, and could count himself lucky if he succeeded in finding his way out again and escaping the ever-present danger of stepping suddenly into a bottomless well, or being struck down in the dark by an unseen yellow hand.

Only the most astute initiate could hope ever to find his way through the complicated system of trap-doors, winding stairways, and rope-ladders which gave laborious access to the spacious apartments where the Chinks live in a splendour that is almost oriental.

While the lives of this cunning, nocturnal people are veiled in mystery, it is known that chief among their activities are the smoking of opium and the enslaving of Pudencians – the latter occupation, in fact, being their only known profession, to the pursuit of which they bring a resourcefulness that cannot fail to fill the mundane student with amazement. All the forces of law and order are, of course, arrayed against them; but, by allying themselves with the most lawless and disreputable elements of the white world, they have been able to go on plying their nefarious trade without abatement.

Just what their object is in enslaving white girls no one seems clearly to know; but it is generally agreed that their purpose is a horrible one, and every Pudencian regards capture by the Chinks as a fate worse than death.

In ordinary circumstances, we should have been at a loss for means of approach to the hidden city of the Chinks. But, fortunately, the same trusty who had informed us of Pansy's fresh peril had given us (in return for a pardon from the governor) the address of a confederate in the underworld, who, he assured us, would pilot us safely through the mysterious subterranean realm. 'Just say to him, "Six feet north and the wind's in the east," ' said the trusty, 'and he'll know you're on the square. He may be a yegg,' he added feelingly, 'but he'll never squeal on a pal.'

On our way to the city we took the precaution to stop at the governor's palatial residence long enough to effect such alterations in our appearance as would enable us to pass unnoticed, in the metropolis. To this end, the governor exchanged his frock coat for a ragged jersey and placed a black patch over his right eye; while I contented myself with the assumption of a false moustache. Thus disguised, we crept out of the gubernatorial mansion, although not without engaging in an altercation with the governor's valet, who mistook us for would-be assassins of his master.

We proceeded, now, to the address which the trusty had given us. The house we sought lay in the most ill-favoured quarter of the town, a wretched district known as the underworld and inhabited by the dregs and outcasts of society. As we wound our way through the narrow, forbidding streets, brutish men scowled and leered at us, and miserable hags – old before their time and scarcely worthy to be called women – showered us with coarse insults. An occasional hurried glimpse, through unwashed panes, revealed a sordid interior in which some sodden lout mercilessly beat a child or a tipsy sailor was obviously succumbing to the blandishments of a scantily clad female whose lineaments bore evidence of the ravages of an evil life. More than once, the governor cast me a look in which horror was mingled with pity, and when the Presence soberly observed, 'The seamy side of the city, where the other half lives and poverty goes hand-in-hand with vice and crime,' the elderly statesman nodded a sad confirmation.

We arrived, at length, at our destination: a dilapidated house, at the foot of a gloomy, tortuous alley, into which the failing daylight scarcely penetrated. We knocked sharply, several times; then we heard the bolts (of which there seemed to be a great many) being drawn, and presently the door opened slowly – but scarcely two inches.

I drew back in alarm as I saw that we were confronting the barrel of a revolver, suddenly swollen to the size of a huge conduit. The next moment I heard an ominous clicking and I feared that our end had come. But fortunately the governor – inured, no doubt, to such experiences – had the presence of mind to utter the magic charm: 'Six feet north and the wind's in the east.' Instantly, the revolver was lowered, the door swung wide to admit us, and a hoarse voice growled, 'Come in.'

We entered a noisome hallway and, as the door closed behind us, we turned to look at our host. A great, hairy face, seamed with evil, glowered at us, and from the twisted mouth came in coarse accents the words: 'I'm Benny the Stump. Who are you and what brings you here?'

He had scarcely spoken these words when an instantaneous inflation of his nether extremities revealed to us that his right leg had been amputated above the knee. A long wooden peg, affixed to the remnant, served as an aid to loco-motion; and it was this appendage, undoubtedly, which had earned for our interlocutor the graphic sobriquet 'Benny the Stump.'

The governor quickly explained the nature of our errand and appealed to our new friend to aid us. At first Benny the Stump sought to dissuade us from our purpose. 'It's ten to one,' he said, 'that you'll never come out alive.' But, when we made it clear to him that we were prepared to court any danger in order to rescue Pansy from her peril, he yielded and, after growling, 'All right. But I warn you that you're playing with fire,' ordered us to accompany him.

He led us to a small door at the rear of the house, which gave access to an alley even narrower and more winding than that upon which the house fronted. Night had fallen now, and, in the dim rays of the street-lamps, we saw mysterious shapes, dodging into obscure doorways or slink-ing down cellar-steps. And, here and there, silhouetted sharply against the drawn shade of a brightly lighted room, we saw, to our horror, an arm that poised a dagger, or a pair of huge, hairy hands that were closing about a woman's slender throat. 'With the coming of night,' observed the Presence, mournfully, 'the forces of the underworld creep out of their holes, and evil stalks through the deserted streets.'

Now and again, a slippered figure shuffled past us, and

for an instant the dim light revealed a yellow countenance and a pair of slanting eyes that regarded us narrowly. 'Chinks,' whispered Benny the Stump hoarsely.

Presently, we came to a halt before a small shop, which gave every evidence of being deserted. But, in response to Benny the Stump's thrice-repeated knock upon the barred doors, we heard the approach of cautious footsteps, and a moment later a little panel in the door slid back noiselessly, and through the aperture a greatly enlarged eye surveyed us malevolently. (I learned, later, that the doors of all dwellings inhabited by members of the dark-skinned races are equipped with sliding panels or lattices, and that it is impossible for any white person to gain admittance to these habitations without having first undergone a severe scrutiny by the custodians of these portals.)

Benny the Stump muttered quickly the open sesame, 'Six feet north and the wind's in the east,' whereupon the door swung wide and we entered the tiny shop. When our eyes became habituated to the dim interior, we saw that our new acquaintance was a most hideous dwarf. He looked at us with suspicious malignance, and his crooked fingers toyed with the hilt of a huge knife, which he carried at his belt.

But as Benny the Stump informed him of our purpose, his snarling distrust gave way to a kind of malicious delight, and his little eyes gleamed with an evil joy. Without more ado, he bade us wait a moment and hobbled quickly into the shadowy recesses of the shop.

Benny the Stump now explained to us that the dwarf, besides being the guardian of the gateway to the underground city of the Chinks, was a half-brother of Wu Long Ti (which, literally translated, signifies the Dragon's Tooth) the powerful ruler of the subterranean yellow world. For twenty years, Wu Long Ti had heaped ridicule and abuse upon his ill-favoured kinsman, until the crooked body of the latter had come to house, beneath its outward submission, a sole, consuming lust for vengeance. So that, fortunately for us, it needed but the statement of our purpose to kindle the smouldering passion of the dwarf into a devouring flame. And while we might, from choice, have linked ourselves with a less unsavoury ally, we were glad in our predicament to employ the tool which chance had thrust into our hands. (The reader will have learned, by now, that chance, in Purilia, has the force of a natural law and that happenings which would strike a human being as extravagantly coincidental are, to the Purilian, the commonplaces of daily life.)

The dwarf returned now with a lighted lantern, and, hobbling to the corner of the shop, pressed his thumb against the eyeball of a joss, whose carven features wore an expression of crafty wisdom. Instantly, a trap-door sprang open at our feet, and we found ourselves gazing into a profound abyss: the entrance to the secret metropolis of the Chinks! Obviously, the governor and I could never by our own unaided efforts have succeeded in discovering it.

Preceded by the dwarf and his lantern, we descended by means of a rotting wooden staircase into the black chasm. From the foot of the steps, our course proceeded through a maze of dim corridors which, I observed, boldly pierced the living rock. A succession of trap-doors, rope-ladders and sliding portals served as impassable barriers to the uninitiated and an occasional glint of steel spoke eloquently of alert, unseen hands.

Several times we passed through faintly lighted chambers, lined with tiers of bunks, in which lay the half-animate forms of yellow-skinned opium-smokers and – I was disturbed to note – more than one white woman, who still bore traces of youthful beauty.

What distressed us even more, however, were sounds of gentle weeping and an occasional glimpse into a narrow cell which housed a fair young girl. These girls, Benny the Stump informed us, were Pudencians who had, in one way or another, fallen into the hands of the Chinks and were being held captive. Many of them, it seemed, were the daughters of elderly aristocrats – often of proud Castilian blood – and had ventured, unaccompanied, into the stronghold of the Chinks, in the hope of somehow averting the financial ruin which threatened their aged parents. Interested as I always was in understanding the economic life of the country, I should have wished to inquire a little more closely into the nature of these financial transactions. But, of course, the circumstances did not admit of such an inquiry; and, indeed, scientific curiosity quickly yielded to concern for these lovely young creatures, immured here in the bowels of the earth and awaiting an unknown fate. (I say unknown advisedly, for to all my eager questions as to just what it was that lay in store for the Pudencians, Benny the Stump replied only with an indubitably significant but – to me – wholly incomprehensible look.) More than once we were tempted to turn aside and attempt to liberate the fair prisoners, but the thought of Pansy's peril held us to our course.

Suddenly, the dwarf extinguished his lantern, and motioned to us to proceed quietly to a grating at the end of the corridor through which streamed a flood of light. We felt our way slowly to the grating, and, as I peered cautiously through, I could scarcely suppress a gasp of astonishment. For the chamber into which I gazed was of such vast dimensions and so sumptuously ornamented that for a moment I doubted the evidence of my senses. It seemed almost incredible that mortal hands could have constructed, far underground, an apartment of such size and elegance. The lavishness of the furnishings could be explained, no doubt, by the indisputably flourishing state of the opium-trade, but the construction of this vast hall in the very heart of the solid rock seemed to me to present a problem in engineering that no earthly, and certainly no occidental, mind could have hoped to solve.

But attention to the business in hand soon banished

speculation, for in the middle of this opulent chamber I discerned the all too familiar figure of Millwood. His evil face wore a sinister expression, which convinced me that he was there for no good purpose. He twisted his moustache repeatedly, and glanced alternately at his watch and at a great carven door at the far end of the apartment. From these manifestations I deduced that he was impatiently awaiting someone. Nor was my inference a mistaken one, for presently the great door opened and there strode into the room a resplendent personage, magnificently arrayed in embroidered silken robes and costly jewels of quaint oriental design.

'Wu Long Ti,' whispered Benny the Stump hoarsely. And from the twisted lips of the dwarf, there issued a snarl of animal hatred.

The dreaded and powerful ruler of the Chinks contemptuously pushed aside, with his foot, the bodies of two of his subordinates, who had prostrated themselves upon his entrance and approached Millwood, who obviously had news of great importance to communicate. Indeed, Pansy's persecutor burst forth, at once, with: 'He's slipped through my fingers again!' At this intelligence, Wu Long Ti evidenced great consternation and plied Millwood with laconic, but importunate questions. I now discovered, to my astonishment, that it was myself to whom Millwood referred. He had learned of my providential escape from the electric chair, and had hastened to bear the tidings to his colleague in crime.

As I scanned their menacing countenances, I became acutely aware of my great peril. It did not need Benny the Stump's muttered, 'They will stop at nothing,' to assure me that my discovery would mean instant death – or worse!

Millwood now produced a folded paper, which he exhibited to Wu Long Ti, outlining, at the same time, in inaudible tones, what I took to be some proposed plan of action. The scheme apparently met with the other's approval, for he nodded his head slowly several times, and a malignant smile lighted his enlarged, saffron features.

When his body became visible again, he clapped his hands smartly together and gave a sharp command (accompanied by a kick) to one of his cringing satellites. The miserable vassal fled the apartment, and I had scarcely time to wonder what mischief was afoot now when the fellow returned, in company with two burly comrades who dragged between them the resistant figure of a white man. As they flung the prisoner brutally at the feet of their master, I saw, with mingled joy and horror, that it was Johnson!

The poor fellow was altered almost beyond recognition. His clothes were torn nearly to shreds, and his matted hair and unshaven chin bespoke weeks of privation and torture. But it was good to know that he was still alive.

At Wu Long Ti's command, Johnson's guards jerked him to his feet, and Millwood ordered him to sign the document which he held in his hand. Johnson glanced at the proffered paper and then, with flushed face and a gesture of refusal exclaimed: 'I'll see you d—d first.'

I experienced an intense desire to know what the document contained when, much to my satisfaction, it swelled to convenient legibility. Imagine my amazement upon ascertaining that it was nothing less than a proposed confession of the murder of Pansy and Mollie by Johnson and me! I could readily understand Johnson's indignant refusal to put his signature to it.

For one dreadful moment I entertained the fear that Pansy and Mollie had actually been done away with by Millwood and the Chinks, and that the two villains hoped to incriminate Johnson and me in order to escape the consequences of their own guilt. But some mysterious inner voice assured me that the girls were still alive, and that the two scoundrels were animated solely by a desire to place us in mortal peril. And, indeed, subsequent events amply confirmed this inner prompting.

Again Millwood ordered Johnson to sign the confession; and again Johnson refused. Wu Long Ti's lip curled angrily. 'If you refuse,' he said, 'it will go hard with you.' Then, seeing that Johnson was adamant, he clapped his hands sharply again and called for one of his chief lieutenants. This subordinate quickly answered the summons. He had the slanting eyes and characteristically vicious mien of the Chinks, but as he was dressed in the trousers peculiar to the whites, I knew him, at once, for a half-breed: a fact which filled me with misgiving, for I had been informed that, owing to some undiscovered chemical law, the infusion of white blood seems to aggravate rather than to diminish the malignant coloured heritage.

My fears were justified almost instantly, for, upon a word from his master, the half-breed produced a leathern thong and proceeded to rain blows upon the defenceless Johnson. Or, at least, so it seemed, for although I saw the whip rise and fall, again and again, and saw, too, the distorted features of Johnson, I was unable to discern any actual contact between the instrument of castigation and the body of its victim. So patent, however, was Johnson's agony that my companions could scarcely restrain me from flinging open the grated door which concealed us, and rushing to his rescue.

When it became obvious, to the two monsters, that the flogging served only to heighten Johnson's determination not to sign the confession, they decided upon new means of persuasion. At a command from Wu Long Ti, the half-breed reluctantly flung aside his whip, and, hurrying from the apartment, returned almost at once with Mollie. I was overjoyed to learn that she was really alive and well; and although it was evident that she had suffered (a fact eloquently attested by two tears, of enormous size and gelatinous texture, which crept slowly down her cheeks) I was glad to note that her sufferings had not been of a nature to impair the bloom of the cheeks themselves, nor to mar either the freshness of her frock, nor the perfection of her coiffure.

The guards curbed the mutual impulse of Johnson and Mollie to fly into each other's arms; and the fruition of Millwood's scheme was arrested long enough to allow Mollie's magnified visage to become the arena of a somewhat protracted display of what I had learned to recognize as evidences of emotion.

Since this work (in intention, at least) is primarily scientific in character and only incidentally the record of a personal experience, I must digress sufficiently to lay before the reader some further general observations upon the emotional life of the Purilians and the singular manner in which it finds expression.

As I have already indicated, the existence of a Purilian is divided equally between violent physical activity and almost equally violent emotional activity. But what I have not perhaps succeeded in making clear is, that the two forms of activity are closely interrelated, and that not only is every physical act fraught with emotional significance, but every emotion is patently evidenced by some external physical manifestation.

It would be reasonable to assume that a people whose life is so largely dominated by the play of emotion would have developed not only a wide and minutely graded emotional range but a complex and varied machinery of expression. The reverse, however, is the case. The emotions of the Purilians are as quantitatively limited as they are qualitatively simple. And although they compensate in intensity for what they lack in variety and complexity, the method of their expression cannot fail to strike the curious observer as singularly undeveloped.

It might be contended that the Purilians, completely absorbed as they are in the life of the emotions, have adopted, for convenience's sake, a sort of emotional shorthand, by means of which a simple symbol connotes, to the initiated, a complex concept. But this hypothesis would be more tenable were there evidence anywhere in the Purilian world of an attempt at social organization or of conscious control of political or psychological problems. And when I add that all my inquiries into the subject were met with the puzzled incomprehension which is the characteristic Purilian response to any abstract question, the reader, I am certain, will share my conclusions.

Suffice it to say then, that there exists, in Purilia, a system of symbolical emotional gestures, which is as rigid and as universal as the ritual of an established church. And, just as the observant visitor to an alien place of worship soon learns to associate certain cadences and genuflections with certain phases of religious expression, although the creed itself may be a mystery, so does the terrestrial observer in Purilia soon learn to associate specific grimaces and contortions with certain emotional experiences of the inhabitants, although the nature of the emotional life, itself, may be veiled in the profoundest obscurity.

I had, therefore, not been long in the country before I was able to recognize, without difficulty, the expression of such feelings as shame, terror, hatred, grief, and the like; a process in which I was greatly aided by the fact that these expressions of emotion are invariably accompanied by a protracted swelling of the subject's features, which affords the beholder more than ample time for their detailed perusal.

In a preliminary study such as this (for this volume pretends to be nothing more) it is impossible to set forth in detail the Purilian system of emotional symbolology. And, indeed, it is a labour which had better be left to the psycho-physiognomist. I shall content myself, therefore, with a brief description of a few examples of these significant facial and corporeal calisthenics in which almost every Purilian is an adept.

Thus, for instance, to shut the eyes tightly (while awake) is an unmistakable evidence of intense suffering. This gesture, however, is confined almost exclusively to women, intense suffering in men being expressed by a parting of the lips and a firm clenching of the teeth. (As I shall try to make clear, not only is this variance in emotional expression a secondary sexual characteristic, but the emotions themselves vary with the sexes as well as with the castes.)

The lowering of the female eyes is a certain evidence of shame; whereas terror is expressed by a frantic clutching of the throat, accompanied by a pronounced protrusion of the eyeballs. To stare vacantly into space is an infallible indication of profound despair (and, I may add, this vacant staring is a practice in which the Pudencians appear particularly expert – doubtless because they are constantly plunged into situations in which despair seems an inevitably appropriate emotion). Dire perplexity is expressed by a repeated manipulation of the brow, with the fingers of the right hand, beginning at the left temple and ending in the middle of the right cheek. In extreme cases, perplexity also loosens several wisps of hair at the front of the head. A Pudencian, in moments of embarrassment, hangs her head, or, if her nature should be slightly frivolous, rapidly taps the ground with her foot.

The appearance of profuse perspiration upon the brow is, in Paragonians, an evidence of profound agitation, but in Vauriens an indication of mortal terror. Females, in Purilia, do not perspire, it being one of the many physiological curiosities of the country that they are not provided with sweat glands. A desire to be reunited to an absent person is always expressed by prolonged staring at the photograph of the distant one; whereas, grief over the mistakenly assumed infidelity of an absent lover finds its happiest expression in the shedding of tears over a vase of flowers (preferably roses and, whenever possible, a bouquet which was the gift of the lover himself).

A Bordellian usually indicates the waning of love by removing her costly jewels and returning them to her erstwhile lover. In cases of extreme revulsion of feeling, the jewels (frequently pearls of extraordinary size) are torn from the throat, and flung at the feet of the lover. For a Bordellian to proffer a man a latch-key is a symbolic evidence of symbolic lust; while, on the other hand, a return to a more virtuous mode of life finds expression in a change of attire from a lacy negligée to a simple street-costume of dark hue.

To talk out of the corner of the mouth is a sure sign of villainy; and, indeed, so patent an evidence of evil intentions is this method of conversation that it is usually employed only by criminals of inferior social position. Vauriens, higher in the social scale, usually give evidence of their sinister intentions by raising their right eyebrows. This may or may not be accompanied by a rolling of the cigar between the lips (depending upon the degree of villainy contemplated). A cigar is unmistakable evidence of an evil nature. When tilted upward, it expresses the happy fruition of some malign intent, and when depressed, at the corner of the mouth, it is an infallible indication of lust (should the eyes be narrowed, at the same time, one may be sure that the lust is unbridled). Paragonians are frequently cigarette-smokers, but the smoking of a cigarette is not in itself evidence of a heroic nature, especially not if the smoker should wear a derby hat or permit a growth of hair upon his upper lip. Pipe-smoking is proof, not only of a kindly and guileless nature, but of paternity. Smoking in women is an infallible evidence of symbolic lewdness and is confined to Bordellians of the most depraved sort.

It may occur to the thoughtful reader that since good and evil in Purilia are so patently stamped upon the exteriors of their possessors, it should be a comparatively simple matter for the virtuous young of both sexes to escape those harrowing predicaments into which I have described them as habitually falling. And, indeed, so at first it would appear. But, as I have already intimated, there is, in Purilia, neither continuity of emotional experience nor a stream of cultural tradition. The individual, absorbed in his or her emotions, leads a singularly isolated life, in which social consciousness appears to play no part. The possibility of rational living seems never to present itself to the Purilian. No attempt is made to educate him in the principles of what most intelligent humans would regard as ordinary sane behaviour. In fact, I am inclined to believe that he is ineducable. Certainly, judged by generally accepted terrestrial standards, the average Purilian is emotionally unstable and mentally defective. In fact, if one were to search for human prototypes of representative Purilians, one might almost confine one's investigations to the institutions for the insane and the feeble-minded.

I confess that the foregoing represents a purely scientific view. Some of my friends who are of a more metaphysical cast of mind and to whom I have recounted my experiences in Purilia have sought to persuade me that the conditions of life there are determined by moral laws, incomprehensible to mere humans, and indicative of a degree of spiritual and emotional evolution to which this planet of ours has not yet attained – and indeed may never attain. Unversed as I am in the subtleties of metaphysics and holding as I do a mechanistic view of the universe, I cannot hope to combat the contention of my more learned friends. I can merely state my sceptical disbelief in their theory, with the added confession that if such moral laws do govern Purilia they are certainly incomprehensible to me.

But it was the man, and not the scientist, who stood concealed, behind the grated door in the underground fortress of the Chinks, and gazed helplessly at the plight of Mollie and Johnson, in the clutches of Millwood and his yellow-skinned confederates.

Millwood, who had been waiting impatiently for the

features of Mollie to resume their normal size, now once more ordered Johnson to sign the confession. Again Johnson refused. An evil smile lighted Millwood's face. Taking his watch in his right hand, and pointing to Mollie with his left, he said to Johnson: 'You'll either sign in two minutes, or — ' I did not hear the alternative, but from Millwood's smile, and from the muffled exclamation of horror which escaped the governor at my side, I knew that the scoundrel was threatening Mollie with a fate worse than death. Mollie, although fully clothed, now crossed her arms and hugged her bosom tightly; an infallible evidence of outraged modesty. Profuse beads of sweat appeared upon Johnson's forehead, and Wu Long Ti fingered his scanty beard in a manner that I knew, by now, betokened lust.

Then the dial of Millwood's watch shut everything else from view, and, for many agonizing seconds, I was obliged to note the progress of the tiny pointer. But at length Johnson, unable to contemplate the spectacle of Mollie being delivered to a fate worse than death, broke down and cried: 'I'll sign!' And, although the confession incriminated me as well as himself, I could scarcely blame him for electing to sign it.

Mollie, temporarily out of danger, cowered in a corner. (I was rather surprised to note a great rent in her sleeve – the result, apparently, of Johnson's having signed the confession.) And, before I could even speculate upon the villains' probable next move, I saw, to my mingled joy and consternation, that Pansy was being dragged into the room. Except for the hurried glimpse of her veiled form in the death-house, it was the first time I had seen her since that memorable night, in her apartment, when Millwood had falsely claimed her to be his bride and I had been dragged off to prison, charged with murder. And, although we were both again in mortal peril, I was happy to see that her imprisonment had not altered her appearance and that she had, in all her misery and danger, found time not only to attend to the innumerable pretty details of her charming toilet, but also to acquire a new and exquisite frock.

Seizing the girl by the wrist, Millwood thrust his face close to hers, and said: 'For the last time, will you marry me?' Confident as I was that Pansy would answer in the negative, I still felt a sense of elation when, shaking her head emphatically, and allowing two large globular tears to roll slowly down her cheeks, she said: 'Not as long as I live.'

Millwood's lip curled in an ugly sneer, and turning to Wu Long Ti he said: 'Then she's yours, to do with as you like.' My astonishment and dismay upon hearing these words were exceeded only by Pansy's, and for a long time she stood there clutching her throat, a prey to the most devastating emotions. Then she looked about desperately for a means of escape. But it was useless; every door was guarded by a vicious Chink, who smiled evilly at her plight. Convinced that she was trapped, Pansy stood in the middle of the vast apartment, hugging her bosom in her folded arms, and watching Wu Long Ti, who approached her with a deliberation that seemed scarcely consistent with his manifest lust. I wanted to burst into the room, but Benny the Stump would not permit it; and I stood looking on, in impotent dismay.

Suddenly, just as Wu Long Ti was about to take the terrified Pansy in his arms, a woman appeared from an obscure corner of the apartment, and, throwing herself at Wu Long Ti's feet, interceded for the girl. The woman's painted cheeks and décolleté evening-gown testified eloquently that her life had not been all that it should have been; and a dark circle beneath each eye gave evidence of her addiction to opium. From the expression of cruel disgust on Wu Long Ti's face, I inferred that the woman was no longer attractive to him, an assumption which the Presence confirmed by announcing: 'Hophead Sue, once Wu Long Ti's plaything, but flung aside now like a worn-out glove.' And, as the Chink chieftain sought literally to fling the woman aside, Benny the Stump gave utterance to a low growl, the significance of which I did not at once understand. Then, as Sue clung desperately to her former lover, the Chink uttered a sharp command and, to my horror, I saw the half-breed lieutenant raise a dagger and prepare to plunge it into Sue's back.

With a great cry, Benny the Stump now threw open the grated door, behind which we lay concealed, and rushing into the room, interposed his body between Sue and the half-breed, in time to receive the descending dagger-thrust that was intended for the woman. As Sue turned and beheld her rescuer, who now lay prostrate upon the floor, she uttered a great cry of startled recognition and with an agonized exclamation of 'Father!' threw her arms about the dying man. Thereupon, Benny the Stump opened his eyes and after rolling them several times in a most distressing manner, whispered hoarsely: 'I guess I'm done for, Sue.'

An inexplicable phenomenon now occurred. For, to my amazement, I found myself suddenly transplanted, from the underground world of the Chinks, to a humble but tidy dwelling which apparently was the former home of Benny the Stump, Hophead Sue, and a sweet-faced Umbilican, who, it seemed, was Benny the Stump's wife and Hophead Sue's mother. Benny, however, was in possession of both legs and appeared to be a sober and respectable artisan; whereas Sue had the semblance of a young and pretty girl (although a superabundance of ruffles upon her frock bespoke a flighty temperament).

There followed, now, a long, incoherent, and confusing series of incidents, carrying Benny the Stump and his family through many varied locales and introducing a great number of unfamiliar persons. Concerned as I was about the fate of Pansy, whom I had last seen in the hands of Wu Long Ti, I fear that I did not give adequate attention to these incidents concerning Benny the Stump and his family. But I did gather that the girl, falling in with evil companions, had somehow found her way into the hands of the Chinks. (All this, apparently, had taken place many years before and I found it extremely bewildering.) It appeared, too, that Benny the Stump, overcome with grief as a result of Sue's disappearance, and giving her up for dead or worse, had taken to drink and to beating his wife. The good Umbilican had succumbed eventually to sorrow and maltreatment; and Benny the Stump, having somehow, in connexion with all this, lost his leg, had gone from bad to worse, until, at length, he had become the desperate denizen of the underworld at whose door we had knocked. But, through it all, he had never surrendered the image of his beloved daughter, always hoping against hope that he would some day be reunited to her. Sue, too, in all her degradation and misery, had cherished the belief that she would one day encounter her venerated father again. And although each now found the other strangely altered, and the circumstances in which they met could scarcely be regarded as auspicious, there was yet a measure of happiness in this belated meeting; and the inference that Benny the Stump died happy in the fulfilment of his dearest wish was unmistakable.

Bewildered though I was by this unexpected and incomprehensible transportation through space and time, I had yet sufficient awareness of my surroundings to observe that I was being suddenly whisked back again to Wu Long Ti's apartment, where Benny the Stump was still in the act of expiring in the arms of his erring but repentant daughter. Indeed, he even managed to defer his demise long enough to bestow his paternal absolution upon the wayward young woman. This act of charity performed, he succumbed. His death was attested by the governor who ceremoniously removed his hat and pressed it firmly against his chest, with the crown outward. This formality, I had learned, is the Purilian equivalent for the medical examination to which we humans are accustomed. And, although the act may be said to be religious rather than scientific in character, it has all the force which we habitually attach in similar circumstances to a physician's pronouncement. (This curious fact serves only to illustrate again how, among the Purilians, our own physical and material values are translated into the spiritual and emotional realm.)

The dramatic intrusion of Benny the Stump into Wu Long Ti's apartment had led, of course to the discovery of the dwarf, the governor, and myself. We were seized and dragged before the ruler of the Chinks, with what seemed to me an unnecessary degree of violence, since we made no attempt at resistance.

I was astonished and rather hurt to note that Pansy gave me no sign of recognition; but a moment's reflection persuaded me that her failure to recognize me could be attributed to my disguise. And, indeed, this was the case, for when Millwood, with a savage sneer, tore the false moustache from my lip, I saw recognition slowly dawning upon the girl's beautiful features. It was a lengthy process, and, as emotion succeeded emotion, even I fell to wondering how long it would be before recognition was complete. Finally, however, she uttered my name and I breathed a sigh of relief.

The half-breed now removed the patch from the governor's eye, whereupon Wu Long Ti, too, underwent a process of recognition, although less extensive than Pansy's. The governor, who represented the forces of law and order, was of course regarded as a dangerous foe by Wu Long Ti (who, in turn, represented the forces of lawlessness and disorder); and the Chink's joy at finding his sworn foe in his hands knew no bounds.

Our situation was truly desperate. Millwood had us completely in his power – not only Johnson and me, but Pansy and Mollie. Held captive as we were, deep in the bowels of the earth, we had nowhere to look for deliverance. Or at least so I believed. For I had not reckoned upon Nature!

Johnson, the governor, the dwarf, and I were now bound hand and foot. At an order from Wu Long Ti, a priceless rug was removed from the floor, and a great trap-door was revealed. In the middle of this cleared space, I was placed together with the other three prisoners. Then, Wu Long Ti, with a malignant smile, turned to Millwood and nodded slowly and significantly. Millwood strode to the wall and, placing his finger against a button, said to Pansy: 'When I press this, the man you love will be – missing.' It did not need either the cries of Pansy and Mollie or the frenzied shrieks of the dwarf to tell us that, concealed beneath the trap-door upon which we stood, lay a bottomless abyss, into which the pressure of Millwood's finger upon the button would plunge us.

I closed my eyes and awaited the end. But, even through my closed lids, I could see Millwood's finger creeping nearer and nearer to the fatal button. Another half-inch and our lives would be snuffed out.

But that half-inch was never spanned. For, suddenly, I became conscious of a great commotion. The apartment was filled with wild cries of alarm, and hastily opening my eyes I saw, to my astonishment, that great fissures were appearing in the walls and ceiling. 'An earthquake!' cried the governor.

And so, indeed, it was! When every hope had perished, Nature had intervened to save us! (I shall have occasion later to write, at greater length, of the part which these natural catastrophes play in adjusting the emotional difficulties of the Purilians.)

But, elated as we were by this unexpected deliverance, we had no time for thanksgiving, for the danger of being crushed to death by great masses of falling rock and masonry was a very real one. It was an earthquake of the utmost severity. The whole ingeniously constructed metropolis of the Chinks collapsed like a house of cards. As for the Chinks themselves, they displayed for so astute a people a remarkable lack of self-possession, confining their efforts at escape to a frantic and aimless rushing about, which resulted only in great numbers of them being buried alive beneath the falling rubble: a just punishment, of course, for the evil which they had practised.

Wu Long Ti, more cunning than the rest, sought to make his way through the wreckage toward some secret outlet. But he had not reckoned upon the despised dwarf; and, as the wily leader of the Chinks moved hastily across the trap-door, the deformed object of his cruelty pressed the button in the wall, and Wu Long Ti plunged to the death that he had designed for us. And as he hurtled into the abyss, a crumbling column crushed out the life of the dwarf himself, an exultant cry still upon his lips.

Naturally, my chief concern was for Pansy, and I tried to make my way to her side through the debris. But Millwood was too quick for me and, seizing the girl in his arms, he flung her across his shoulder and sped along a corridor. I tried to pursue him, but, to my despair, a collapsing wall barred my way.

Johnson, meanwhile, was endeavouring to rescue Mollie, but, almost as he reached her side, she disappeared beneath a mountain of falling plaster, beyond any hope of deliverance.

We were in despair. Our lives had been saved, but the two young women for whom we had risked them were far from safe. Indeed, Mollie was buried alive, and Pansy was being borne off, no one knew where, by a man who had demonstrated that he would stop at nothing. (I should add, too, that in the confusion attendant upon the disaster, we had completely lost sight of the governor and were reluctantly compelled to give him up as lost.) I had just succeeded in persuading Johnson that we had best make our escape from the underground realm when my ear caught a low moan which, I soon discovered, emanated from Hophead Sue, who lay dying under a mound of masonry. As I bent over her, she looked up at me and said; 'I guess you think I'm a pretty bad lot, don't you?' I hastily reassured her upon this score, whereupon she drew my ear close to her mouth and whispered: 'Millwood is sailing to-night on the Southern Cross.' Having uttered these words, she expired.

Johnson and I, in accordance with the custom of the country, removed our hats and then, having performed this rite, proceeded to make our escape. It was no easy task. Never had I seen such heaps of rubbish; but we succeeded at last in finding our way to the surface again. We were delighted to remark that the earthquake had been entirely subterranean. The aspect of the city was unchanged, and the catastrophe apparently had had no other effect than the salutary one of wiping out the stronghold of the vicious Chinks.

CHAPTER 15

THANKS to Hophead Sue's opportune dying utterance, we were provided with a definite clue to Millwood's whereabouts; and, hurrying to the nearest steamship office, we succeeded in procuring passage upon the Southern Cross, which was indeed sailing that night.

In fact, as it lacked but a half-hour of the ship's sailing-time, we entered a taxicab and ordered the driver to take us to the pier as speedily as possible. In our haste, it did not occur to us to inquire into the character of the driver, who, as events soon proved, was one of Millwood's hirelings. Indeed, our suspicions were quickly aroused, for we perceived that the taxicab, instead of proceeding in the direction of the dock, was speeding through the outlying districts of the city toward the open country. We ordered the driver to stop, but he merely quickened his speed; and we knew by the evil grin which he turned upon us that we had fallen, once more, into the hands of our arch-foe.

Our vehicle sped along a deserted country road until, at length, it drew up before a tumble-down shack, from which emerged a half-dozen desperadoes, armed to the teeth, who seized us roughly and dragged us toward the hovel. Undaunted, however, Johnson lunged forward violently and, scattering our captors right and left, ran to a tree near by to which two saddle horses happened to have been made fast. I followed, and, before our enemies had time to collect their wits, we had untied the horses, mounted them, and turned their heads towards the city.

In a few moments, we heard the sound of a motor behind us and, looking back, saw that the bandits had crowded into the taxicab and were in hot pursuit.

It was obviously an unequal race; but nevertheless our horses managed to hold their own, and, although the bullets whistled about our ears, fortunately none of them took effect. (Luckily for the orderly element in the Purilian population, poor marksmanship is almost always a concomitant of villainy.) My previous adventures in Purilia led me to believe that we were in for a long chase; and I was not mistaken. The pursuit led up hill and down dale, around sharp curves, across rickety bridges, and through crowded thoroughfares, our horses still gallantly maintaining their lead.

At length, one of the bullets of our pursuers did take effect. I felt my mount quiver beneath me, and all at once he collapsed in a heap, and I fell heavily to the ground. But Johnson's presence of mind saved me. Wheeling quickly, he reached over and, seizing me about the waist, drew me almost from under the wheels of the pursuing taxicab, on to the saddle behind him. A touch of Johnson's foot, and the splendid animal was off again, with the bandits' automobile close at his heels.

For many more miles, the chase continued until, after a time, our steed began to weary under his double load, and as the pursuers crept ever closer and closer it seemed that our capture was inevitable. But again deliverance came from an unexpected source. As we clattered across a drawbridge, that spanned a turbulent river, the draw unexpectedly began to open. Our horse, by a great leap, just managed to carry us safely across the widening gap. But our pursuers were less fortunate; for unable to apply their brakes in time, they were precipitated into the whirling rapids beneath.

This danger happily averted, we resolved to make another desperate effort to reach the Southern Cross. I looked at my watch and saw that it lacked but three minutes of sailing-time; and the sudden colossal apparition of a steam whistle, from which numerous jets of vapour escaped, convinced me that the hour of sailing was indeed near. The upsetting of a fruit-vendor's cart and several other minor incidents of a similar nature delayed us only momentarily; and all went well until, at the very entrance to the steamship dock, we found our way barred by the passage of a long freight train. But our indomitable mount gathered his haunches, leaped high, and cleared the freight train, with scarcely an inch to spare. Then, with a final burst of speed, he dashed the length of the pier and up the rising gang-plank on to the deck of the ship, much to the astonishment of the officers and passengers.

As we dismounted, our goal attained, I saw Millwood leaning against the rail, watching us with narrowed eyes, a cigar clenched at a sinister angle between his lips. Of Pansy there was no sign, and I wondered what the scoundrel had done with her. But several days were to elapse before we learned news of her.

By terrestrial standards, the voyage was an eventful one. There were several mutinies, a sanguinary encounter with a pirate ship, a desperate fight, with knives, between a brutish sailor and another member of the crew (who turned out to be a young nobleman travelling incognito in order to remove a blot from his family name); the murder of a card-sharper by one of his confederates; and the theft of some priceless gems of quaint oriental design from the cabin of a Rajah (who was travelling incognito in pursuance of a scheme to to destroy the supremacy of the white race and carry off a Pudencian who had excited his lustful fancy). But, accustomed as I had grown by now to seeing through Purilian eyes, I knew that these happenings were merely the normal incidents of a sea-voyage.

For most of the passengers, the voyage was brightened considerably by the presence on board of an unusually stout lady and her travelling-companion (who was one of those maladjusted little men, with ill-fitting trousers, to whom I have already referred). This pair furnished considerable amusement to the other passengers, by virtue of the fact that they appeared to be chronic sufferers from sea-sickness, a complaint which, among the Purilians, is regarded as highly comic. And lest this view of an ailment, which, among us, is deemed singularly unpleasant, should strike the reader as odd, I had best attempt to set forth some further observations concerning the physiology and the pathology of the Purilians.

As I have already explained, the Purilians, while bearing outwardly a close physical resemblance to the inhabitants of the earth, have a physiological constitution which is infinitely less complex than ours. Not only are they devoid of a reproductive system, but (with such exceptions as I shall note) they lack a digestive system as well. The absence of all this complicated apparatus naturally relieves them from the innumerable organic disorders to which we mortals are subject; and it can be truthfully said that as a people the Purilians enjoy an immunity from disease which may well give us less fortunate humans occasion for envy.

Such diseases as occur are found, usually, only among the lower orders of the population: and by lower orders I mean, of course, those persons whose emotional life cannot be regarded with any degree of seriousness. And since it is only the serious emotional life that is deemed worthy of respect and sympathy, it is not to be wondered that the ailments of those who do not live upon this plane should be regarded with levity. I am unable to state authoritatively why disease should be more frequent among the lower orders than among the higher; but I assume that, as the Purilian advances in emotional profundity, he comes to live more and more in a spiritual zone, in which corporeal disabilities are unknown. Or perhaps it is that the high-caste Purilian's susceptibility to wounds, bruises, contusions, fractures, and swoonings has bred in him or her an immunity to organic disease. Certainly, it is difficult to see how any organism could endure our own common illnesses in addition to the abrasions and maimings which the ordinary Purilian suffers almost daily. (I should add that, fortunately, these wounds heal with astonishing rapidity and without leaving disfiguring scars.)

But, whatever the reason, the fact is that the Purilian victims of organic disease are not only persons of low station but objects of mirth, as well. In addition to sea-sickness (of which I have already spoken), influenza, in all its forms, invariably provokes merriment. All its ordinary symptoms, such as sneezing and coughing, are conducive to great hilarity. I am quite within the facts when I say that no Pudencian, Paragonian, or Umbilican has ever been known to sneeze. (This might argue an absence of the respiratory system, as well as of the generative and digestive, were it not for the anomaly that, not infrequently, a Pudencian falls victim to pulmonary consumption. This, it is scarcely necessary to add, far from provoking mirth, occasions profound grief.)

Delirium tremens, by us regarded as a malady of the utmost gravity, is a source of unfailing delight to the Purilians, especially when accompanied by hallucinations of a zoological character. Inflammatory disorders, particularly gout, are also a source of much good-natured amusement. Sufferers from this latter disorder are easily recognizable.

The ailment, which always settles in the right foot, is treated by swathing the diseased member in voluminous bandages. The victim is then provided with a cane, by the aid of which and with the additional assistance of his hand upon his left hip he makes painful and precarious progress. Invariably he has the misfortune to encounter some hasty individual who treads heavily upon the injured foot, and hurries on without a word of apology or a backward glance. This, of course, causes the sufferer to hobble after the offender, in attempted pursuit, brandishing his stick and filling the air with imprecations, a spectacle which always moves the onlookers to extravagant mirth.

To be afflicted with parasites is also considered comic. The same may be said of maladies of the teeth. The latter always result in the swelling of the victim's jaw to prodigious size. Tying the face in a large handkerchief, which is knotted upon the crown of the head, the sufferer rushes frantically about in search of relief, usually upsetting elderly persons, breaking several windows, and becoming involved in an altercation with a policeman in baggy trousers, in his efforts to find alleviation of his pain. Eventually, he succeeds in making his way to a dentist's office, and (after protracted waiting) in gaining access to the practitioner, from whom he demands instant relief. As is the case with other branches of science, dental therapy in Purilia is not in an advanced state. The customary method of dental extraction is for the practitioner to place his knee upon the chest of the patient and, without administering any anaesthetic, to remove the affected tooth violently from the jaw by means of a large pair of forceps. The diseased teeth are invariably of abnormal size and so deeply embedded in the jaw that the force of extraction frequently propels the dentist through the wall of his establishment and into a barrel of tar which, for some inexplicable reason, is always on the sidewalk just beneath.

In addition to these ailments, persons of low caste are

constantly subject to mishaps of a decidedly painful nature, which, however, are by universal acceptation essentially comic. Among these risible minor disasters are violent blows upon the head (particularly those resulting in optical illusions of an astronomical nature); loss of footing, due to contact of the pedal extremities with fruit peels, ice, or some other lubricous substance; rents in the apparel of the nether extremities caused by enraged canines; bullet-wounds in the gluteal region; the loss of false hair in a sudden gust of wind; and the accidental gulping of artificial teeth.

There are, however, several diseases which are regarded as being dignified and to which members of the higher castes are not infrequently subject. Chief among these are heart failure and apoplexy, both of which are deemed highly respectable and worthy of the expenditure of a good deal of emotion. The symptoms of these two ailments are almost identical. The victim opens and closes his mouth several times in rapid succession, rolls his eyes, and then slumps heavily, either upon the floor or into a chair. If the attack is particularly acute, he dislodges a vase in his fall, or else clutches at a table-cloth, with a resultant breakage of crockery. Now and then a Paragonian falls victim to temporary blindness, but happily this dreadful affliction is always completely cured by a simple operation, the exact nature of which I was unable to learn. Another extremely common ailment is temporary loss of memory, but of this I shall have more to say, in another place.

In a land so happily free from disease one should scarcely expect to find medical science highly developed. And indeed its state is almost primitive. Time is regarded as the sovereign remedy for all wounds, and, although this concept may strike the terrestrial reader as mathematical rather than clinical in its implications, its therapeutic soundness is unquestioned by all good Purilians. Physicians and nurses do exist, but their function seems to be more aesthetic and emotional than medical. The patient appears to find curative powers in the contemplation of the doctor's well-trimmed beard and the nurse's carefully arranged tresses rather than in the application of their remedies. It is true that the clinical thermometer and the stethoscope are known to the Purilians, but their use apparently is entirely ritualistic.

It may well be that the retarded state of medical science in Purilia may be explained by the fact that spiritual and metaphysical forces play an important role in restoring to health the sick and disabled. Many a curative miracle is wrought by the application of faith and love, unaided by medicament or surgical appliance. The efficacy of prayer has been demonstrated, again and again, by cures of a nature which could not fail to strike wonder into any human of scientific inclinations: these devotional exercises being particularly successful in restoring power of locomotion to adolescent females (a class of persons peculiarly susceptible to paralysis of the lower limbs).

After we had been at sea for some days, I happened to learn that Pansy was on board ship, but was being held prisoner by Millwood. This important piece of information I obtained as a result of overhearing a conversation between Millwood and the ship's chief officer (who, it seems, was one of his tools).

When I first learned of Pansy's incarceration I was greatly disturbed, for I assumed that Pansy was being detained in Millwood's cabin, and that her honour (synonymous in Purilia with chastity) would be endangered. But, to my great relief, I learned that Millwood had provided her with a separate cabin. This act struck me as a little quixotic in an arch-scoundrel – especially since he had taken such pains to abduct her – but, apparently, neither he nor his fellow conspirator seemed to regard this circumstance as being in the least odd.

Having learned the location of Pansy's cabin, I managed now and then to catch a glimpse of her and, from her appearance, I gathered that she divided the hours of her imprisonment equally between quiet weeping, and painstaking attention to her toilet.

From overhearing several further conversations between Millwood and the perfidious first officer, and from finding a number of highly revelatory notes which Millwood in his careless way dropped promiscuously about the deck, I learned, too, that not only were the pair engaged in a plot to sink the vessel for the insurance money, but that they were plying the ship's master with poisoned liquor in order that they might inherit his fortune (by virtue of a will which they were busily engaged in forging) and at the same time cast suspicion upon him of a murder which the chief officer had committed.

Armed with this information, Johnson and I held a hasty conference and determined to inform the unsuspecting captain of what was afoot. But, unfortunately, Millwood and the first officer happened to overhear our discussion and resolved to put us out of the way at once.

Accordingly, we were waylaid by a half-dozen most villainous-looking seamen, with scarred faces, and belts that bristled with naked knives. The ringleader of these ruffians was an ill-favoured giant, known to his fellows as Bloody Dick, whom we had seen, on more than one occasion, bend an iron bar double and who was easily a match for any three of his comrades.

Johnson and I were bound hand and foot and dragged to the stern of the vessel. 'You're goin' to visit Davy Jones's locker,' said Bloody Dick grimly, as he hoisted us upon the rail: a sally which caused his comrades to roar with savage laughter. We were ordered to say our prayers, before we were deposited into the surging billows beneath us, and I closed my eyes, in anticipation of the end.

But a great shout caused me to open them again. Johnson, fortunately for us, had suddenly recalled an old wrestling-trick, which he had learned in his boyhood. Placing his fore-finger under Bloody Dick's left arm, he gave a mighty heave and tossed the giant sailor over the rail as though he were a feather. This unexpected end of their leaders' career threw the other scoundrels into momentary confusion, and Johnson and I, taking advantage of the uproar, slipped out of our bonds and took shelter behind one of the lifeboats.

Undoubtedly, we should have been ferreted out in a very few minutes, but a storm, which had been gathering for some time, now broke, and the sailors, in their consternation giving thought only to their own safety, left us to our fate.

That the apparently fortuitous advent of the storm was a direct intervention in our behalf, upon the part of Nature, we could not doubt. And lest the reader believe either that he has not read aright or that our adventure had, by now, undermined our reason, I must endeavour to make clear to him the relationship in the Purilian universe between the forces of Nature and the private lives of the Purilians.

Accustomed as the reader is to regarding Nature as a blind, implacable, and untamable force, to whose vagaries man must accommodate himself as best as he can, he will find it difficult to understand a natural order in which catastrophes familiar to us – e.g., floods, conflagrations, volcanic eruptions, and the like – not only are timed by Nature to resolve the difficulties of some worthy Purilian but behave with such discriminating consideration that their dire consequences are visited only upon the evil.

I have already described the fortuitous advent of the earthquake, in the world of the Chinks; and, if the end it achieved seems to the reader incommensurate with the gravity of the disaster, it is only because no human can fully understand the overwhelmingly important role which spiritual love plays in the Purilian scheme of things. I cannot state too often nor too emphatically that everything, even Nature, is subordinate to it; and, by Purilian standards, the razing of a forest or the devastation of a countryside is a small price to pay for the happy union of a beautiful Pudencian and a brave Paragonian. One's view of Nature, in Purilia, cannot be other than anthropomorphic, for with true philanthropy, she does not hesitate to use freely her dreadful arsenal of flood and fire and thunderbolt to bring about the adjustment of some difficulty in the emotional life of a well-favoured Purilian. It is literally true in Purilia that the stars in their courses fight for the triumph of spiritual love.

Consequently, we looked upon the storm as a happy omen, for although we could scarcely regard ourselves as favoured children of Nature we assumed that the elements took a kindly interest in the welfare of Pansy, and that this tempest was somehow designed to advance the best interests of her emotional life.

Our elation, however, soon gave way to despair, for, in a very few minutes, it was noised about that the ship was sinking. Even in my dismay at this alarming intelligence, I could not escape a feeling of surprise that so palatial and apparently so seaworthy a vessel should succumb in such brief time to the ravages of a storm which seemed to me only moderately severe. But, no doubt, the captain's drunkenness, Millwood's villainy, and the fraudulent schemes entailing the insurance-money and the forged will, all contributed to the sudden dissolution of the stout vessel.

(I learned, subsequently, that the hazards of sea travel in Purilia are, if anything, greater than those attendant upon travel by land. Scarcely a ship reaches the port of her destination – although why this is so, I was unable to discover. As I have already remarked, marine architecture appears to be highly developed and storms, while frequent, are apparently mild and of brief duration. I think it likely that incompetent seamanship is largely at fault. As nearly as I could make out, the masters of vessels are all either unprincipled scoundrels, bent upon the execution of some malignant design, or else they are kindly old gentlemen of rather feeble intellect, who become the easy dupes of sinister conspirators. Many of them, too, have beautiful daughters, whose emotional difficulties tend to take the minds of their devoted fathers from the serious and arduous business of navigation.)

My first thought upon learning that the vessel was breaking up was to look about for some means of escape. And in this natural desire to avoid annihilation I assumed that I should have the co-operation, not only of my fellow passengers, but of the officers and crew. But, to my astonishment, no attempt was made to use the life-saving equipment with which the ship was provided, and, far from looking to their safety, the passengers gathered, *en masse*, in the principal saloon and knelt in pious attitudes, while the ship's band (which seemed to have undergone considerable augmentation during the progress of the storm) spiritedly struck up a religious air.

It needed, now, but one more flash of lightning to sink the ill-fated vessel, which speedily disappeared beneath the waves, leaving no trace but a few floating spars. Fortunately, as I came to the surface I observed Pansy struggling about in the water not more than six feet away. Lashing her to a spar, I managed to keep her head above water, and, as we floated about in the waves, I was pleased to see that Johnson was clinging to another bit of wreckage not far away.

The storm subsided, now, as quickly as it had arisen, and, as the clouds cleared away, we saw the sun sinking magnificently; and near at hand, to our unspeakable joy, stood revealed an inviting beach, with a line of stately palm-trees sharply silhouetted against the darkening sky.

A few strokes more and our feet touched bottom. I helped Pansy up the sandy beach and as we stood there, saved from the storm, I was delighted to note that she had emerged from the water as fresh and unspotted as though she had stepped from some dainty boudoir. Such purity as hers, I concluded, was impermeable even to the harshest of the elements.

Johnson now joined us, and we made our way toward

147

some native huts in the distance, happy in our deliverance and reunion. We should have been less elated had we known that Millwood, at the first indication of the tempest, had made his escape in one of the ship's boats and was already plotting our undoing with the native chieftains.

CHAPTER 16

Our first days upon the tropical shore afforded a welcome relief to the arduousness of our sea-voyage. As the Presence aptly phrased it: 'A few days of sunshine and air made the world look a little brighter.'

We were well received by the chief of the natives, a great bearded man, wreathed with flowers, every square inch of whose body was covered with intricate tattooed patterns. Deceived by the chief's hospitality, we did not suspect that he was plotting against us and we allowed ourselves to be lulled into false security.

During the relatively eventless days which followed, I had ample opportunity for making observations upon the natural conditions of the Purilian tropics and of the physical characteristics and social life of the inhabitants.

The vegetation in these regions consists almost entirely of palm-trees, and these are invariably arranged in majestic rows along the horizon. It is a remarkable feature of the landscape that no matter where one looks one is almost certain to see a line of these stately trees, standing up sharply against the sky. For the rest, the tropics consist chiefly of long stretches of smooth, sandy beach, which afford a convenient arena for the choreographic exercises of the natives, to which I shall have occasion to refer again presently.

Except for an occasional herd of charging elephants, the fauna of the tropics consist almost entirely of monkeys and parrots: the former displaying a remarkable propensity for indulging in all sorts of amusing antics, and the latter being particularly adept at mimicking the speech of the white residents (especially such utterances as are scurrilous or profane in character).

The natives are, superficially, a simple childlike people, but actually capable of the most perfidious treachery and appalling bloodthirstiness. Physically, they are tall and handsome, the females being, for some unknown physiological reason, several degrees lighter in colour than the males. Their dress is simple, consisting of a grass skirt, a tight-fitting sleeveless cotton shirt, a floral wreath and coral ornaments. Despite the simplicity of their attire, however, the women have developed the use of cosmetics to a remarkably high degree, and their well-tended hands and feet and carefully blended complexions afford an interesting contrast to the primitiveness of their attire.

Occupationally, there is a sharp sexual cleavage. The males divide their time between beating the tom-tom and engaging in sanguinary submarine battles with man-eating sharks. The women (who seem never to survive their twenty-second year) spend all their time in dancing upon the sandy beaches. Indeed, the entire communal life of the natives may be said to centre about these terpsichorean exercises.

The dances, which all the whites agree are highly improper, struck me as being models of decorum. Indeed, I was surprised to remark that, upon a few occasions when a slight tinge of eroticism crept into the monotonous gyrations of the dancers, their performance came to an abrupt end, and one found one's attention focused upon a line of palm-trees, along the distant horizon. I could only surmise, therefore, that the impropriety in these natives dances is symbolical and that, since the dark-skinned peoples of Purilia are notoriously incapable of experiencing spiritual love, any evidence upon their part of sexual emotion must be set down as lustful and hence highly reprehensible and offensive to all right-thinking persons.

Since my major interest is ethnology, the reader will forgive me if I enter, at this point, into a brief discussion of the ethnic situation in Purilia. And, indeed, no one can hope to attain to even a partial understanding of that remarkable land without becoming first acquainted with the inter-relationships of the several Purilian races.

The civilization of Purilia is predominantly a white civilization, despite the vastly numerical superiority of the dark-skinned races. This dominance of the whites is explicable partly by the fact that they are white and partly by the fact that (as I cannot repeat too often) they alone, of all the peoples in Purilia, have the capacity for spiritual love.

Unfortunately, however (and owing, no doubt, to their heavier pigmentation), the dark-skinned races persist in a stubborn refusal to recognize the obvious superiority of the whites. Naturally, this results in unremitting conflict between the white race and the coloured races: the latter persisting wrong-headedly in declining to accept the logical alternatives of submission or extermination, which are offered them by the former.

The terrestrial reader can form no adequate conception of the number of wars, insurrections, revolts, forays, sorties, ambuscades, massacres, abductions, conspiracies, and machinations, to which these racial conflicts give rise. The outposts of white civilization are in a constant state of warfare and turmoil: the dark-skinned races (or natives, as they are called) being in no sense deterred from their efforts to throw off the white domination by the fact that there is no recorded instance of any of their uprisings being in the least degree successful.

In view of what I have already said concerning the numerical superiority of the natives, the thoughtful reader may regard it as singular that they should always be doomed to defeat. But this is readily explained by the fact that practically any white is worth ten natives, either in pitched battle or in hand-to-hand encounter. Furthermore, since, in every one of these conflicts which was brought to my attention, the emotional life of a Pudencian was, in some way, involved, the genius which presides over the lives of these lovely young women saw to it, no doubt, that the outcome was a happy one.

To make credible to the reader the extraordinary fact that beautiful young women invariably become involved in political and racial struggles of the kind I have described, I should explain that all native rulers, without any exception whatsoever, from the most petty chieftain to the most magnificent potentate, are dominated by lust and, in all their political activities, are animated solely by a desire to possess some beautiful Pudencian. A record of the toll of life which the relentless pursuit of these base passions has taken would make unpleasant reading indeed!

One of the most needed reforms in Purilia, in my opinion, is the invention of a system which would prevent the Pudencians from falling into the hands of the native chieftains. Nothing could go further toward the establishment of universal peace than some effectual method of curbing the propensity of the Pudencians for walking, unwittingly, into the nets which the native rulers are constantly spreading for them. Whether because their own innocence makes it impossible for them to suspect duplicity in another, or because (as, I fear, is the case) their intelligence is not always on a parity with their virtue, the fact is that the beautiful young creatures are simply not to be trusted to themselves within a thousand miles of a native ruler. I tried to discuss this problem with a number of prominent Purilians, but, as always, they displayed little or no interest in the consideration of a general problem, and I was forced to the conclusion that the needed reform could be brought about only by education – although this process is, of course, inevitably a slow one.

(I should add that the foregoing observations upon the dark-skinned races do not apply to the Negroid peoples. These, as I have already pointed out, are essentially a comic folk, temperamentally incapable either of questioning white superiority or of experiencing lust.)

Another curious anomaly may be found in the deplorable fact that the white residents of the territories occupied by natives, far from elevating their dark-skinned inferiors to their own high level of white excellence, show a lamentable tendency to sink to the depths of depravity in which the natives habitually dwell. Whether this moral disintegration is due to the palm-trees, the dancing girls, the charging elephants, or a combination of all three, I was unable to ascertain; but, whatever the cause, there exist in these tropical regions vast numbers of men who have sullied their splendid white heritage and have allowed themselves to sink into abject native degradation. Caught in the toils of some native Bordellian (usually a stoutish dancing-girl), they consume unbelievable quantities of vile liquor, refrain from shaving, and pick quarrels, over trifles, with their erstwhile beloved comrades. Fortunately, many of them are saved from complete disintegration by the advent of some crisis which reawakens in them the all-but-extinct spark of white manhood and stirs them to the commission of deeds of prodigious valour, whereby they rehabilitate themselves in the eyes of the whites, resume the habit of shaving, and win the love of some beautiful Pudencian. (The native Bordellian, the reader will be happy to learn, almost invariably perishes ignobly.)

I had been only a few days in the tropics, when I encountered upon a beach a young member of the class I have just described. Although he was attired in miserable rags, I guessed at once, by his handsome features and rather black expression, that he was a Paragonian. I soon scraped up an acquaintance with him, and we became quite friendly, although he steadfastly refused to reveal his name. 'Just call me Fred,' he said. Bit by bit, I learned his story. He was the son of a noble family, who because of certain circumstances (the nature of which, I confess, I did not clearly understand) had been wrongfully accused of a murder of which he was entirely innocent. A few simple words of explanation would have cleared him of the charge, but he could not have spoken those words without compromising a woman's fair name; and, although the woman in question was no better than she should have been, he naturally preferred disgrace and exile to behaving in a manner unbecoming to a Paragonian.

So he had come out to the tropics under a cloud; and, sinking lower and lower, had finally been forced to resort to beach-combing, a mysterious occupation, which barely supplied him with the means to procure the enormous quantities of alcohol that constituted his daily ration.

My friendship with Fred was to bear the happiest results for Johnson, Pansy, and myself. After we had been, for some little time, on this tropical shore, Millwood and the native chief who had been secretly plotting against us decided that the time was ripe and prepared to strike. I happened to learn of their plans, by overhearing a conversation between them, and, having warned Pansy and Johnson, we attempted to make our escape. A long chase through the jungle ensued, which, in its essential outlines, resembled the innumerable other long chases to which I had been subjected since my arrival in Purilia. Finally, we were captured, bound hand and foot, and carried back to the native village.

The next day was to be a feast day (which, among these people, is celebrated by the beating of tom-toms and prolonged dances upon the beach); and one of our guards informed us that we were destined to be the victims of a nameless fate. What that fate was to be, the reader may well imagine.

We lay all night in the compound, awaiting the dreaded morrow. I tried to snatch a few moments' sleep, but the incessant beating of the tom-toms made it impossible. Early next morning, we were startled to see a figure crawling rapidly toward us, through a breach in the wall of the compound. It was Fred! (How he had managed to elude the innumerable armed guards with whom the place was beset I was never able to discover.)

We hastily informed Fred of our peril, and after the lapse of a decent interval, during which he displayed the emotions appropriate to the situation, he informed us of his intention of summoning aid. To this end, he purposed to swim to a settlement some miles distant, which was equipped with a wireless station, by means of which assistance could be procured. It seemed a heroic but foolhardy undertaking, and we sought to dissuade him. 'But the danger!' said Pansy. 'They would stop at nothing.' But Fred was not to be deterred and, after shaking hands all around, he set off upon his dangerous mission.

The reader, by now, is no doubt sufficiently familiar with the Purilian scene to supply for himself the details of the pursuit which followed. Fred's detection, as he entered the water; the launching of the pursuing canoes; the narrow escape from the jaws of a shark; the hurled spears, which just missed their mark; the swimmer's exhaustion; the submerged rock that, not a moment too soon, sank the frail native craft; and the friendly hands that pulled the all-but-dead youth to safety: all these succeeded each other in orderly fashion.

Meanwhile, we three were dragged out of the compound and tied to palm-trees, in the middle of a circle of savage-looking natives. There we stood, bound and helpless, awaiting our unknown fate. Millwood now appeared, and, once again, offered marriage to Pansy, promising not only to release her but us as well, if she accepted. But the fine girl proudly refused. Finding her still obdurate, Millwood raised his hand high. We fastened our eyes upon it, for we knew that, when it fell, it would be the signal for our end. An interminable time elapsed, during which the faces of the savages expanded and shrank, one by one giving us ample opportunity to observe the bestial cruelty that disfigured every countenance.

Then we saw Millwood's hand again, still poised. One second more and it would fall. But before that second had elapsed, the sound of distant guns threw Millwood and his savage allies into consternation. 'The marines!' cried Millwood. And, at these dread words, he and his cohorts broke and fled to cover.

Millwood's surmise had been correct; the marines had indeed arrived. Fred's frantic call for help, speeding through the air, on waves of ether, had brought the brave fellows rushing to our rescue. It was a heartening sight to see them charging along the beach, setting fire to the native huts and slaughtering the cowardly savages by the hundreds. When they had finished their splendid work of extermination, only a few smouldering embers and a heap of dark-skinned bodies remained to tell of the erstwhile stronghold of savagery.

Fred had accompanied the marines, and Johnson and I now pressed forward and wrung his hand in gratitude. But, when I urged him to return home with our rescuers, he shook his head and replied: 'Not until I have cleared my name.' At these words, an officer of the marines stepped forward and grasped Fred by the hand. The officer, it seems, was a former classmate of Fred's, who had been commissioned by the government to find Fred and bring him back home. It appeared that the true murderer had confessed his guilt upon his death-bed, completely absolving Fred of any complicity in the crime. Fred, of course, was delighted to learn that the stigma had been removed from his name and that, once more, he could take his rightful place in the world of white men. And when the officer added, with a significant smile, 'And Mary told me to say that she'll be waiting for you,' the cup of Fred's happiness was full.

While we were yet rejoicing, however, we saw steaming along the horizon a yacht which we recognized as Millwood's. And when we directed the officer's binoculars to the vessel we saw, to our dismay, Millwood upon the deck, with Pansy beside him. In the confusion attendant upon our rescue, the fellow had managed to smuggle Pansy away and was now making good his escape. We hastily explained Pansy's danger to the officer, who, with characteristic courtesy, placed a government cruiser at our disposal; and, before many minutes had elapsed, we had set off in pursuit of the unprincipled Millwood.

CHAPTER 17

IN the course of the days which we spent upon the cruiser, in company with the marines, we had ample opportunity to observe these splendid warriors and to learn, as well, many interesting facts concerning Purilian warfare and the details of martial life.

The marines, as a body, are, beyond question, the finest group of males that it has ever been my good fortune to encounter anywhere. Handsome and of splendid physique, they have a prepossessing exterior matched only by their military prowess, their intrepidity, their exquisite sense of honour, their chivalry, and the loftiness of their sentiments and ideals. From this description, the reader will surmise correctly that the professional military service in Purilia, far from attracting the dregs and derelicts of society, draws its recruits from the finest flower of Purilian manhood.

Nor should this occasion wonder. For the conditions of war in Purilia are such that any (white) young man who takes up the profession of arms is certain of an opportunity not only to perform deeds of amazing valour, but to win, as well, the hand of a delectable Pudencian. True, he must be prepared to undergo the most extraordinary ordeals; but what youth possessed of a spark of manhood would flinch from that, especially when he has the assurance of emerging covered with honours, and the certainty that the wounds and privations which he must endure will leave neither blemish nor ill after-effects?

Warfare in Purilia is conducted much more pleasantly than among us, presenting few of the distressing aspects which make our terrestrial armed conflicts so abhorrent. The disease, the filth, the racking agonies, the wanton destruction, the unloosing of bestial passions – all these are happily unfamiliar to the Purilian martial scene.

The wars are brief, spirited, and full of lively and entertaining action. All engagements are decisive ones and end in the ignominious rout of the enemy. (The enemy – as I have already explained – is, in almost all instances, a dark-skinned people that has challenged the supremacy of the whites. Occasionally, however, one finds whites pitted against whites; and, in these cases, the enemy is the people that does not happen to speak the prevailing language of Purilia – which, as the reader will have inferred from the examples of Purilian speech I have cited, is a quaint variant of our own English tongue.)

Much of the fighting – especially in the wars against natives – is in the open, consisting of spectacular hand-to-hand battles (in which, as I have indicated, the whites are always outnumbered, at least ten to one) or in the storming of fortified positions that appear impregnable, but, nevertheless, yield readily to the onslaught of the whites, whose casualties are negligible compared to those of the defenders.

When trench warfare is employed, its rigours are alleviated by the splendid recreational opportunities which are afforded the men under arms. Indeed, these warriors lead a happy, carefree existence, in which good wine, jolly comradeship, and high-spirited but wholesome fun combine to relieve the tedium of life in the trenches. The non-commissioned officers are, without exception, droll fellows of humble origin (and with distinctly comic emotional lives) whose exuberant antics serve to refresh and hearten the Paragonians (who are always either privates or commissioned officers – the inevitable promotion from the ranks invariably carrying with it a commission).

In addition, the scene of battle is always brightened by the presence of the Pudencians, who are constantly found in large numbers in the very forefront of action, sometimes as nurses, but more frequently merely in the capacity of (emotionally) interested spectators. Their presence, far from impeding military operations, serves as a spur to the martial ardour of the soldiers. And their neat appearance and cool freshness, in the midst of shot and shell, might well serve us earthlings as a model of behaviour upon the field of battle.

All in all, then, warfare in Purilia is a fine, vigorous, high-spirited, sportive activity. There is never any troublesome political or economic issue involved, such sources of conflict being happily unknown. All wars are righteous wars, achieving the salutary objective of exterminating some people which does not think cleanly about the Pudencians. It is not to be wondered, therefore, that every Umbilican, consumed, as she is, by maternal love, considers it her proudest privilege to consecrate her son (usually an only one) to a career that offers such unequalled opportunities for the display of heroism and chivalry and the wearing of apparel which sets off the male figure to its best advantage.

For some days, after leaving the tropical shore, we kept Millwood's yacht in sight; but one night, in a heavy fog, we lost her and were unable to pick her up again. We cruised about for many hours, scanning the horizon in vain for some trace of the vessel. At length, the captain of the cruiser, who had just received word of an insurrection among some desert tribes, declared that he could no longer delay. But he had hardly given the order for the cruiser to put about, when one of the seamen dashed into the cabin, bearing a bottle he had happened to observe bobbing up and down in the waves close to the ship.

Upon investigation, it was found that the bottle contained a note in Pansy's hand, divulging the fact that Millwood's destination was the gold-mining country in the far north (where, it seems, he had extensive claims) and imploring the finder of the bottle to come to her rescue.

It was a lucky chance which guided this important missive directly into our hands; and, the captain of the cruiser, in answer to our entreaties, obligingly agreed to delay putting down the insurrection until after he had conveyed us to the shore for which Pansy was bound.

Arrived in the northland, the captain bade us a cordial farewell, and sent us ashore in one of the ship's boats. We sought to persuade him to allow a detachment of marines to accompany us, in the event that help would be needed in rescuing Pansy. But this the captain sorrowfully, but firmly, declined to do – not because of a lack of interest in Pansy's welfare, but merely because a nice question of military punctilio was involved. It seems that the duty of rescuing Pudencians, in the region where we now were, belonged by tradition to the mounted police of the district, and that these latter, sensitive of their military prestige, would have considered it an affront if the marines had encroached upon their prerogative. When the matter was made clear to us, we could do nothing but endorse heartily the captain's decision and express our admiration of the fine sense of honour which prompted it.

We found ourselves now in a land of ice and snow, where, as the Presence expressed it: 'Nature seldom smiles and even the stoutest hearts sometimes quail, until, spurred on by the golden lure, they take up the bitter struggle anew.' It seemed to snow incessantly, and the roads, piled high with drifts, were passable only by means of dog-sledges. At sunset, one could see great numbers of these sledges proceeding along the crest of a distant ridge, their dark outlines sharply silhouetted against the sky.

The inhabitants of this land are all men of colossal stature, and, although statistics were unobtainable, I am certain a survey would establish the fact that the average height of a gold-miner is at least six inches greater than the general average of the Purilian population. Not being a biologist, it is impossible for me to say whether or not the connexion between tallness and gold-prospecting is genetic or merely accidental. Curiously enough, however, one finds scattered among this titanic population, a number of those strange little men (whom I have previously described), who seem as unsuited to this environment as to any other, and who exhibit here an almost tragic propensity for consuming, unwittingly, the breakfast of a particularly large and savage gold-prospector, walking unawares into the den of a ferocious bear or tossing about, with supreme carelessness, large packets of explosives.

The region is a mountainous one and is, we were led to believe, rich in mineral deposits. (As one elderly prospector expressed it: 'Thar's pay dirt in them thar hills.') But, although there was much bustling about and going back and forth, it all seemed, to the casual observer, to have very little relation to gold-mining. Indeed, nowhere could I find any evidence whatever of mining activity, nor did I see how it was possible to keep the land clear of snow long enough to penetrate even the surface of the soil.

There was, however, much emotional activity. Many of the miners had come out under a cloud; others were wanted by the authorities; and yet others had come because they wanted to forget. In some cases, the Pudencians, who were always at the source of these mining expeditions, found their way to the gold country and, naturally enough, distracted the attention of the miners from the laborious task of delving for the precious metal. But, in most cases, the miners spent their time in gaming and drinking, until the receipt of news from home assured them that the particular difficulty which had caused their departure was cleared up, and that it was practicable for them to return to the Pudencians, who had discovered that they had gravely misjudged the absent ones.

(A word should be said concerning the sledge-dogs, in which the region abounds. These animals not only often equal their masters in intelligence, but lead emotional lives of remarkable intensity. They are heroic and self-sacrificing to a degree to which many humans might well hope to aspire; and the feats of devotion they perform are well-nigh unbelievable. Many a Pudencian and Paragonian have these noble animals to thank not only for their happy union, but for their very lives.)

Most of the activity of the region centres about the large dance-halls, which are the most prominent feature of every settlement. 'Here,' as the Presence explained, 'Dame Fortune and the Demon Rum take their heavy toll and sin rears its ugly head.' And whenever one entered one of these infamous resorts, one was certain to find in progress a drunken brawl over a game of cards; a fight to the death, with knives, for the possession of the favours of some pretty dancing-girl; or the attempted murder of a Paragonian by a band of ruffians, who sought to rob him of his mining-claims.

We made the round of these resorts in the hope of finding some clue to the whereabouts of Millwood and Pansy. But all our inquiries elicited nothing, until, one night, chance took us to a particularly disreputable bar-room, known as the Red Dog. As we stood at the bar and ordered our drinks (which, in accordance with the custom of the country, were swallowed at a gulp and in rapid succession) my attention was attracted to one of the bartenders, a fine-looking youth, who seemed singularly out of place in these rough surroundings. Too, there was something strangely familiar about his appearance. Somewhere I had seen those features. But where I could not recall; nor could Johnson aid my recalcitrant memory, although he, too, recollected having seen the boy's face before.

While we were still trying to establish the identity of the lad, a great bearded prospector strode into the resort and, after brushing the snow from his eyebrows, advanced to the bar, smote it with his gloved fist and, addressing the youth, bellowed: 'Gimme a whisky and make it quick, you — !'

Although I did not hear the epithet uttered, I could tell by the man's expression that he had called the lad's paternity into question. The boy's eyes flashed fire and, drawing his revolver, he levelled it at the burly ruffian and exclaimed between his set teeth: 'When you say that, smile!' For a moment, the prospector stared at the lad in incredulity, and then, as he saw the forefinger ready to press the trigger, his features broadened into a great grin. Instantly, the boy lowered his revolver, the two shook hands heartily, and the prospector insisted upon the young man joining him in a friendly toast.

Then, all at once, I recognized the youth. He was Charlie, the long-missing brother of Pansy, over whose photograph we had seen Mrs Malone shed so many tears of yearning! I communicated this startling intelligence to Johnson, and his opinion corroborated mine. We eagerly addressed the boy, speaking of Pansy and of his mother's anxiety concerning his safety. But he merely stared blankly at us. It was evident that he did not understand a word of what we were saying. All our efforts failed, and we should have remained completely mystified by the boy's strange behaviour, had not the Presence obligingly explained: 'Amnesia, caused by a blow upon the head, had made Charlie lose all recollection of his former existence, and chance, or some unknown force, had directed his wandering footsteps to the gold-fields.'

We saw, now, that it was useless to attempt further conversation with Charlie until he had been cured of this malady. In the course of my inquiry into the pathology of the Purilians, I had obtained a great deal of information concerning amnesia, which is one of the few ailments to which dignity attaches. It is a common disorder and, as far as I was able to discover, is always the direct result of a blow upon the head. The victim, his memory completely destroyed, always feels an irresistible impulse to journey to some remote and inaccessible region and to engage in some occupation totally alien to his former mode of life. There is only one known remedy for the disease, namely, a second blow upon the head, which invariably results in instantly restoring the sufferer's memory and awakening in him a yearning to return immediately to his distracted relatives.

Johnson and I retired to a table in the corner of the bar-room, and debated our course of action. While we were convinced that a sharp blow upon the head would restore Charlie, the remedy seemed so drastic that we hesitated to administer it. We were still weighing the pros and cons of the matter, when an elderly man in the dress of a prospector sat down beside us and greeted us courteously. Johnson and I almost sprang from our seats in startled recognition. The elderly prospector was none other than the governor!

But he turned only a blank face to our eager questionings, and it soon became obvious that he, too, was a victim of amnesia (caused, as we correctly surmised, by falling masonry during the earthquake), and that chance (or some unknown force) had directed his wandering footsteps to the gold-fields.

We were still marvelling at the governor's presence here and rejoicing that, at any rate, he was still alive, when our attention was attracted to the rude stage at the end of the bar-room, upon which a dancing-girl now appeared. Judge of our amazement when we saw that the girl was none other than Mollie.

Apparently, then, she had not been buried alive by the earthquake, as we had believed, but had merely been stunned by falling masonry (for it soon became obvious, from the blank stare with which she regarded us, that she too was a victim of amnesia).

While Johnson and I were still deliberating upon the most effective means of restoring Mollie, Charlie, and the governor to an awareness of their true identities, the door of the bar-room swung open again, and the fur-clad figure of Millwood strode into the room. Shaking the snow from his great bearskin coat and brushing the congealed flakes from his eyebrows, he walked up to the bar and ordered a drink. Then, as he was about to raise the glass to his lips, he happened to glance at the large mirror behind the bar, and saw our reflected images. For a long moment he stared at the mirror in incredulity; then the cigar fell from his lips, and the half-raised glass dropped from his nerveless fingers, and was shattered into a thousand fragments upon the floor.

Slowly, he recovered the semblance of composure, and, turning away from the bar, made his way deliberately across the room to where we sat. It seemed to take hours for him to weave his way among the crowded tables, his figure looming larger and larger as he neared our corner.

We knew that he regarded his present situation as a desperate one, for not only did his face wear a look of grim determination, but we heard the Presence observe: 'Realizing that his game was almost up, Millwood resolved to stake everything upon his last card.'

We had not long to wonder what that last card might be, for, pointing an accusing forefinger at us, Millwood turned to a great bearded fellow, who sat at an adjoining table, and said: 'Sheriff, arrest these men. I charge them with the murder of Pansy Malone and Mollie St Clair.'

This announcement threw the crowded room into an uproar, and, as we sprang to our feet in indignant denial, the occupants of the other tables swarmed about us. Apparently impressed by the earnestness of our protestations of innocence, the sheriff (whose badge of office, a highly polished five-pointed metal star, was prominently displayed upon the lapel of his coat) turned to Millwood and demanded proof of the grave charge he had made against us.

Millwood, undaunted, merely smiled and said: 'I've got proof enough to send them to the chair.' And, taking a folded paper from his pocket, he handed it, with affected nonchalance, to the sheriff. As the sheriff opened the paper, we saw to our amazement that it was the confession which Johnson had signed, in the apartments of Wu Long Ti, in order to shield Mollie from the improper advances of the Chinks.

The sheriff read the confession through and then, shaking his head gravely, said: 'Looks purty bad to me.' We protested our innocence again, explaining the circumstances in which the confession was signed, and offering as irrefutable proof of the truth of our story the fact of Mollie's presence in the very room in which we stood. But this apparently convincing proof of our innocence actually led to our complete undoing, for Mollie, upon being questioned, denied having ever seen us before, or having any knowledge of the facts which we had recounted – so far afield had the unhappy girl's misfortunes caused her mind to stray!

In the minds of the sheriff and the bystanders, there was now not the least doubt of our guilt. And whatever hope we may have entertained of establishing our innocence before a properly constituted tribunal soon vanished, too; for we quickly learned that there was to be not a moment's delay in bringing us to trial, but that we were to be subjected to the summary frontier justice which prevails in these remote glacial regions.

In less than five minutes, a jury was impanelled from among the bearded giants who surrounded us. And, in another five minutes, the evidence was presented and we were pronounced guilty and condemned to be hanged, forthwith.

Nooses were now placed about our necks, and the sheriff opened his lips to order us to be led forth to execution. But, at this moment, Mollie, in whom our imminent peril apparently had awakened some faint stirrings of memory, cried, 'Stop!' and hurried across the room towards us. Then, suddenly, she faltered, swayed for a moment and fell heavily to the floor, striking her head against the edge of a table.

The men gathered about her and soon restored her to consciousness. She opened her eyes and, looking about, gasped: 'What has happened? Where am I?' Then she uttered a shriek of terror as she saw the now unfamiliar bearded faces that bent over her (for the blow she had suffered had completely restored her memory).

She now recognized Johnson and me, and, apprised of our danger, corroborated our story. For a moment, the tide seemed to be turning in our favour. Our judges were obviously impressed by Mollie's recital. But Millwood was not so easily defeated. Nodding his head with affected sympathy, he turned to the sheriff and said gravely, 'Just delirium – caused by the shock.' This diagnosis so impressed our mercurial judges that they again ordered the execution to proceed at once.

But as we moved towards the door in the midst of our executioners, the attention of everyone was attracted by the sound of whining and scratching at the portal. The door was flung open, and a superb sledge-dog dashed into the room, panting with exhaustion, his thick coat glistening with particles of frozen snow. The sage beast soon made it clear to us that someone was in dire need of succour. In the face of this emergency, our execution was temporarily postponed and, leaving us in the custody of Millwood and two or three stout fellows, the sheriff and the prospectors set off behind the dog, who could not curb his impatience to lead the way to the object of his solicitude.

Some hours elapsed – hours which we believed to be our last – and then the men returned bearing with them the unconscious form of a young woman. And, when the recumbent figure was placed upon a table, we were amazed to see that it was Pansy.

Restoratives were quickly applied, and before long, she opened her eyes and, looking about, said faintly: 'Where am I? What has happened?' Informed as to her whereabouts, she proceeded to tell her story. Millwood, it seems, still determined to force her into marriage, had kept her closely confined in his cabin in the hills. For days she had vainly sought some means of escape. But that morning Millwood had left her alone, and her opportunity had come. He had taken the precaution to lock the door of the cabin behind him, but, for some reason, he had overlooked the fact that the window offered a convenient means of egress.

No sooner had Millwood departed than Pansy had succeeded in making her escape, and had set out for the distant settlement. But before she had gone far, it began to snow. Soon the trail was obscured, and, numb with cold and blinded by the whirling flakes, she had wandered about for hours, until, at last, she had sunk exhausted into a snow-bank, where she undoubtedly would have perished had not the heroic sledge-dog learned of her danger and hastened to summon aid. (Fortunately, too, the snow of the region is of a peculiarly dry character, and hours of exposure to it had in no way marred the daintiness of Pansy's appearance.)

Pansy's story completely exonerated and vindicated us, and popular feeling was now directed against Millwood. Seeing that he was defeated at last, he sought to slip out unnoticed, through a door at the rear of the bar-room. But he found his way barred by Charlie and the governor. For a moment, he seemed about to surrender. Then, suddenly, he seized a chair and, swinging it high in the air, brought it down, successively, upon the heads of Charlie and the governor. They fell unconscious to the floor, and Millwood, drawing his revolver, fired at the single oil-lamp which illuminated the bar-room, and plunged the place into complete darkness.

A scene of prolonged and unparalleled confusion ensued. There was much overturning of furniture and a great deal of indeterminate hustling about. When light and order were, at length, restored, it was seen that Millwood had escaped.

Happily, however, both Charlie and the governor emerged from their coma, with their memories completely restored; and there followed many affecting scenes of joyous recognition and reunion.

Our trials now were almost ended. But there still remained

Millwood. We suspected that it was his intention to hurry back to the Malone homestead with all possible speed, evict the poor woman from her beloved hearth, and rob her of the valuable oil-deposits. Our one hope was to arrive at the homestead in advance of Millwood. Accordingly, our party (consisting of Mollie, Pansy, Charlie, the governor, Johnson, and myself) set off at once, in a determined effort to frustrate this last desperate scheme of the scoundrel who had caused us all so much inconvenience.

CHAPTER 18

OUR return journey was a lengthy and arduous one and, as the attentive reader of these pages will readily believe, not free from incident. But I shall make only passing reference to the floods, the avalanches, the tornadoes, the mine-explosions, the bursting dams, and the forest fires which impeded our progress and imperilled our lives. Nor shall I recount, in detail, the innumerable deeds of heroism, the frustrated villainies, and the happy reunions and reconciliations which were the incidents and the fruits of these catastrophes. And, although the damage to property was appalling and the waste of natural resources incalculable, the price was not too high for the triumph of virtue and the uniting of pure and happy hearts.

For some days, we traversed a mountainous region of impressive grandeur. Great ranges, covered with vast virgin forests, unrolled unceasingly before our eyes, in panoramic splendour. And, owing no doubt to some peculiar quality of the atmosphere, it seemed to be always twilight.

A closer view of these mountains belied their apparent isolation and impenetrability. For over every deep gorge leaped an intrepid horseman; in every cañon, a youth dangled by one hand from a slender rope; and upon the edge of every precipice a Paragonian and a Vaurien were locked in a battle to the death. Shots filled the air, pursuits wound their way among titanic boulders and immemorial trees; Umbilicans wept silently, as their thoughts turned to their absent sons, and Pudencians lowered their eyes and clutched their throats, as soberly and as whole-heartedly as if they had been on board ship, in the streets of the metropolis, or in the palace of some native ruler. I was deeply impressed. Here was a people that had bent nature to its will and, refusing to allow itself to be overawed by the terrible majesty of mountain and forest, had persisted proudly in that free play of the emotions and that frenetic physical activity which was its splendid birthright.

We left the mountains behind at length, and entered upon a vast expanse of prairie-land: a great region, devoted principally to the grazing of cattle. Or, at least, so we were informed. But I must confess that I was not fortunate enough to see any of the multitudinous herds which are the reputed source of the economic life of the region; except, now and then, at sunset, when a score of bullocks might be seen proceeding slowly, in single file, along the ridge of some distant eminence, their bodies darkly silhouetted against the sky.

It was not our intention to interrupt our journey for the purpose of visiting this interesting territory. But an enforced interruption compelled us to spend several days there and resulted in the appalling tragedy which it now becomes my painful duty to recount.

One evening at dusk, our train, which had been proceeding at high speed across the prairie-land, came to an abrupt halt, with a suddenness that almost threw us from our seats. An investigation disclosed the fact that the railroad-bridge across a rapid torrent, which lay just before us, had been dynamited. That this was the work of one of Millwood's agents, bent upon preventing our return, there was not the slightest doubt. Fortunately for us all, the young daughter of the custodian of the bridge had learned of its destruction, just a few moments before the arrival of our train. There was, of course, no time to telegraph a warning of the impending disaster. Indeed, our approaching train was already rounding a curve and speeding toward what appeared to be certain destruction. For a moment, the girl stood staring helplessly at the advancing locomotive. Then, with rare presence of mind (and heroic disregard for modesty) she divested herself of the red flannel petticoat which she happened to be wearing, and, rushing to the side of the tracks, waved the garment frantically. The locomotive-driver, correctly interpreting the girl's gesture as an indication of danger, quickly applied his brakes and brought the giant locomotive to a stop within six feet of the dynamited bridge. The girl's ready wit had saved us all from certain death in the roaring rapids.

As it was evident that several days would elapse before the needed repairs to the bridge could be made, there was nothing for us to do but spend the interval in one of the innumerable small towns of the vicinity. Accordingly, we proceeded to the nearest of these, more than a little disheartened by this fresh obstacle, but grateful that Millwood's plot against us had had no more disastrous conclusion.

The town in which we now found ourselves (and which, I may say, was indistinguishable from all the other towns of the region) consisted of a single street of rude, wooden structures, nearly all of which were saloons, dance-halls, or gambling-houses. There was but a single hotel, and to this our party repaired.

The clerk, having assigned us rooms, summoned the porter and ordered him to attend to our baggage. There was something strangely familiar about the porter's appearance, and all at once I recognized him as Jim Slocum, the Malones' hired man, whom we had last seen, months before, at the circus.

At first, I assumed, upon finding him here so far from his

native place, that he was a victim of amnesia. But, as he speedily and joyfully indicated his recognition of all of us, I saw that I had been mistaken and that, happily, none of the severe blows upon the head which I had seen him receive had had any ill effect.

As Jim made his way up the rickety staircase, laden with baggage, his foot caught in a hole in the carpet, and he was thrown forward. As a result, the baggage flew about in all directions, one particularly heavy piece, unfortunately, being hurtled over the banister and descending, with great force, upon the head of the hotel-clerk just beneath. The clerk, stunned by the blow, brought down his fist upon the desk with such violence that the contents of the ink-bottle arose, in a great fountain, and spread over the face and clothing of an acidulous spinster who was in the act of signing the register. The outraged lady raised her umbrella (which she happened to be carrying), with the intention of bringing it down upon the head of the unfortunate clerk. But, blinded by the ink, she missed her objective and struck, with great force, an unoffending elderly gentleman who stood just behind her. The violence of the blow caused the gentleman to stagger backward and collide with a waiter who happened to be passing at that moment, bearing a tray piled high with dishes, with the result that the entire tray-load was deposited upon a notoriously desperate character who was seated at a desk in the act of composing a letter. A great deal of confusion ensued; and as we ascended to our rooms we saw Jim, the clerk, the spinster, the elderly gentleman, and the waiter pursuing each other down the street, closely followed by the outraged desperado, who discharged the contents of two enormous revolvers, right and left, as he ran – to the great terror of the town's inhabitants.

We soon learned, however, that this free and reckless use of firearms is characteristic of the region. The cow-herds, who comprise the bulk of the population, are always well armed, each man habitually carrying at least two revolvers of heavy calibre. At first, this martial display seemed to me inconsistent with an occupation so apparently peaceable as the custodianship of domestic cattle. But I soon learned that cow-tending is merely the nominal pursuit of these warriors, their principal business being the putting down of outlawry and the distentanglement, by force of arms, of the emotional difficulties of the Pudencians, in whom the district abounds.

(Occasionally, too, these doughty fellows are called upon to check insurrections among the Injuns, a dark-skinned people of uncertain origin, who display a lamentable tendency to question the domination of the whites – who, by the laws of nature, are the rightful sovereigns of the region. Sometimes, little bands of embattled cow-herds are so hard pressed by the Injun hordes, that only the timely arrival of a detachment of cavalry or of a squadron of aeroplanes saves them from annihilation. An interesting feature of this petty warfare is the conflagration of the dry herbage of the prairies, which is its inevitable accompaniment.)

The cow-herds, besides being men of superlative courage, are superb marksmen and horsemen. And, despite the apparent paucity of cattle, the industry is evidently a lucrative one, for the cow-herds, in addition to disporting themselves in costly garments of fine silk and handsome leather, with rich trappings of fur and silver, have always a ready supply of cash, which they spend freely at the bar and the gaming-table.

They are, on the whole, a good-humoured and playful lot; and, in the intervals between insurrections, spend much of their time in simple wholesome sports, such as riding their horses through the plate-glass windows of bar-rooms; persuading visitors from the more effete urban centres to dance, by the amusing process of discharging their revolvers at the feet of the strangers; and performing convolutions, with the nooses of raw-hide which form an essential part of their equipment. This latter pastime is an unfailing source of delight to these simple children of Nature, chiefly, I believe, because it induces the flow of a homely philosophy, which finds expression in gently humorous observations, more or less epigrammatic in character.

Would that, with this brief description of the cow-herds, I could leave the subject and pass on to other matters! But my narrative, alas, must now concern itself with the tragic end of Johnson, in this pastoral community.

Readily admitted to the open-hearted and open-handed fraternity of the cow-herds, Johnson and I spent the greater part of our enforced sojourn in one or another of the little town's numerous bar-rooms, enjoying the playful antics of the citizens or witnessing their grim, and often bloody, combats.

On the very eve of our departure, while Johnson and I were standing before the long bar in the most frequented of these resorts, a desperate character of the region, known as Killer Evans, entered the place, in the usual way, through the plate-glass window, and, without checking his spirited horse, leaned out of his saddle and snatched from Johnson's hand the glass which the latter was about to raise to his lips. Then, with a derisive laugh, he leaped upon the bar, and drained the glass, while Johnson, in his effort to avoid the plunging hoofs of the horse, stumbled and fell to the floor.

Killer Evans laughed again, and Johnson, his eyes blazing with anger, arose and, looking up at the mocking figure perched upon the bar, exclaimed: 'You — !' The epithet which he employed, in his justifiable indignation, was one which cast doubt upon the honour of Killer Evans's mother, and, as the ill-fated word was uttered, a gasp and a shudder ran through the crowded bar-room.

Then, to my horror, I saw Killer Evans's hand go to his holster and withdraw a revolver, of unusual size, which he levelled at Johnson. Grasping Johnson's arm, I shouted: 'Smile, Johnson, smile!' And for a moment, I experienced relief, as I saw Killer Evans's trigger-finger relax. But poor, hot-blooded Johnson would not heed my warning. Indeed, it seemed as though I had only added fuel to his anger. Glowering at the menacing figure above him, he ejaculated, 'Smile, hell!'

The words had scarcely left his lips before the poised finger of Killer Evans pressed the trigger, and Johnson fell. I bent over him, hopeful that his wound was not a mortal one, but, before I could even loosen his clothing, the uncovered heads of the bystanders told me that Johnson was dead. A medical examination, now, could have served no purpose other than to confirm what was already a certainty.

So, in the full flower of his manhood, perished my friend and comrade. Together, we had weathered the most unbelievable perils; and now, because in a moment of rashness, he had refused to observe a simple formula, he lay lifeless upon the bar-room floor, a victim to the rigid and immutable Purilian code. A wretched end indeed to so gallant an adventure!

CHAPTER 19

WE delayed our departure one day more, in order that we might see justice done to Johnson's slayer. In the confusion that followed the murder, Killer Evans had escaped; but a committee of indignant cow-herds was speedily organized and, headed by Charlie (who would yield the leadership to none), set off in pursuit of the murderer. After a long and arduous chase, the committee succeeded in running down their quarry, upon the edge of a precipice. The murderer refused to surrender and fired repeatedly at his pursuers, wounding Charlie severely. Despite his wound, however, the brave boy insisted upon attacking the desperado single-handed, and, for a long time, the two engaged in a death-struggle, upon the very brink of the sheer precipice. At length, however, Killer Evans made a fatal misstep and went hurtling over the escarpment, to a merited death.

This act of justice performed, our little party resumed its homeward journey. Charlie's wound healed quickly, thanks principally to the loving care of Mollie, who, even in the hour of her deepest grief, could not forget the needs of others. Indeed, as I watched the large round tears coursing slowly down her cheeks, while her tender caressing of Charlie's head restored to soundness his injured leg, I learned to master my own deep sorrow.

We arrived at the Malone homestead, not a moment too soon. Indeed, as we drove quickly up the road toward the little rose-covered cottage (for, although it was now autumn, the roses were still in bloom) we saw several labourers, under the direction of Millwood and the rascally lawyer, Billings, removing the furniture, while Mrs Malone stood by looking on, her woollen shawl drawn tightly about her thin, stooped shoulders and the large tears coursing slowly down her furrowed cheeks: as heart-rending a spectacle as I have ever looked upon.

The effect of our arrival was magical. The meeting between the aged Umbilican and her beloved son can better be imagined than described. Even Nature seemed to rejoice in the reunion; for the sun, until then obscured, suddenly burst through the clouds and cast a shining aureole about the heads of the devoted pair.

Another reunion, almost equally touching, between the good woman and her long-absent daughter followed; and, yet another, between Mrs Malone and the governor, who, through all the years, had remained faithful to the memory of his early love.

All this rejoicing, however, gave Millwood and his unprincipled satellite, Billings, a chance to slip away unnoticed; and, suddenly, we were all startled by the sound of their powerful car speeding away down the road. Determined that this time they should not succeed in escaping justice, Charlie, the governor, and I jumped into our own car and set off in pursuit. I assumed that we were in for a long chase, and I was not mistaken. A dozen times, some annoying accident seemed to give the wretches an opportunity to elude us; but always we managed to pick up the trail again.

At length, we came out upon a long stretch of open road. Ahead of us was Millwood's speeding car. And, as mile followed mile, the distance between us widened, for we could not hope to keep pace with his costly and powerful vehicle. It seemed as though he were destined to elude us, to the very end.

But that poetic justice which presides like some beneficent goddess over Purilia was not to be denied. Millwood, apparently, had been drinking heavily, and, as he saw us falling farther and farther behind, he could not resist the impulse to turn in his seat and hurl a drunken taunt at us. But his moment of triumph was the moment of his undoing, for, as he turned to resume the wheel, his hand faltered, and the speeding car swerved, struck a tree at the side of the road with great force, and was hurled over an embankment to the rocks beneath.

When we arrived a few moments later at the scene of the accident, we found Millwood's lifeless body, in the midst of a twisted mass of wreckage, which, singularly enough, bore not the least resemblance to Millwood's car. Billings, badly hurt, was taken into custody, and we had the governor's assurance that justice would deal rigorously with him.

The force of the collision had scattered the contents of Millwood's pockets, and I was happy to find among the wreckage not only Mrs Malone's wedding-ring, which Millwood had put to such base use, but the stolen letter containing the money which Pansy's uncle had sent for the payment of the rent. So that I turned away from the scene with the secure feeling that the misfortunes of the Malones had come to an end and that better days lay in store for them.

Among the crowd that had gathered at the scene of the accident was a strangely familiar figure, who came forward and grasped my hand heartily. It developed that he was none other than George St Clair, Mollie's father! It seems that, wearying of circus life and having engaged the affections of the respectable proprietress of a boarding-house, he had united himself to her in wedlock and had become a sober, dutiful, and industrious husband. With pardonable pride, he now introduced his wife to us: a stoutish middle-aged woman, in a rather comical bonnet. They were both delighted to hear that all was well with Mollie and gladly accepted our invitation to accompany us back to the Malone homestead.

It was a happy group that gathered around the supper-table that evening. We were all in high spirits, and even the memory of Johnson could not greatly diminish our jubilation at the happy outcome of events. The meal was further enlivened by St Clair's remarkable lapses in table etiquette and his good wife's obvious disconcertment; and by the ludicrous mishaps which were constantly befalling Jim, who, overcome by nostalgia, had found his way back to his old home and was once more functioning in the capacity of serving-man.

After dinner I asked Pansy to walk with me in the garden, and the readiness of her acquiescence led me to believe that my hopes were not groundless. We made our way to a little arbour, which was flooded with moonlight of extraordinary brightness, so that I was fortunately enabled to study every changing expression of her greatly enlarged countenance.

I sat close beside her and gently placed my hand upon hers. She suffered it to remain, merely lowering her eyes in sweet, maidenly modesty. Then, summoning courage, I put my other arm about her shoulders and drew her slowly, but firmly, toward me. She nestled her head against my shoulder, then, opening her lovely eyes, looked up at me and said: 'I didn't know you cared – like that.'

I assured her that I did; and, convinced apparently that I spoke the truth, she carefully inclined her neck, so that her right cheek pressed against my left one and, with the thoughtful deliberation of an innocent girl about to receive her first kiss, advanced her lips slowly and gracefully toward mine, as the moon cast the brightest of its beams upon her.

We agreed that our happiness must not be deferred and decided that we should be married next morning, by the local clergyman. Our hearts swelling with happiness, we walked hand-in-hand, back to the little cottage. And as we neared the doorway, we saw standing, upon a little mound, a young man and a young woman. He had his arm about her shoulders, and, as his right cheek pressed against her left one, their lips met in a loving kiss. The flooding moonlight revealed the features of Charlie and Mollie. And, apparently fearful that I should deem Mollie disloyal to the memory of my dead friend, the Presence observed: 'Time had served to soften Mollie's sorrow and a new image had come to take its place beside the loved one in her heart.'

The sound of footsteps upon the gravelled path now caused us to turn our heads; and, to our great joy, we saw the aged figures of Mrs Malone and the governor, coming slowly down the path toward us. He had his arm about her stooped shoulders, and she was looking happily up into his rugged old face, while the falling rose-petals fluttered down upon them, in the bright moonlight. I was overjoyed to see that the fidelity of a lifetime had not gone unrewarded and that the widowed head had found a faithful breast to lean upon, in its declining years.

I kissed Pansy good night, and retired to my room, thrilling with present happiness and with the expectation of bliss yet to come. The deep mystery in which the nature of the Purilian marriage relationship was enshrouded served only to heighten my exhilaration. For, in all the months that I had been in the country, I had been unable, despite my most determined efforts, to learn anything concerning the post-nuptial state. In the course of my ethnological researches upon the earth, I had learned, either at first hand or from unquestionably authentic sources, of the existence of an almost infinite variety of marriage customs, covering, I thought, the entire range of personal and social relationships and habits. And yet I had seen enough of Purilia to know that its institution of marriage must be unlike anything that existed upon earth. But what, then, was it like? I had no clue, and so I could only wonder!

As I lay, open-eyed, upon my bed, my brain teeming with these and kindred speculations and with tender images of Pansy, I became slowly conscious for the first time in many months of the ever-present music and the curious rosy tinge of the atmosphere. Constant exposure to these natural phenomena had dulled my senses to them. But now they impinged upon me again. Never, it seemed to me, had the swooning melodies spoken in such mellow and pervasive accents; never had the atmosphere appeared so palpably pink.

Suddenly, I was seized with an unaccountable desire to flee, with a passionate longing to tread again the familiar earth. And, at the same moment, the desperate resolution formed itself to carry off Pansy and fly back to the world with her. I tried to dismiss the project as an idle fantasy; but it would not be shaken off. Indeed, it dominated me more and more, until it grew into a consuming purpose.

I must ask the reader to believe that the course of conduct upon which I had now determined was totally foreign to my nature. In ordinary circumstances, I not only am opposed to hasty and quixotic action, but am reasonably considerate of the rights and desires of others. Yet, in all this, it did not occur to me to take into account what might be Pansy's wishes in the matter. On the contrary, I was quite prepared to overcome, by force and cunning, any objection which she might raise. In self-justification, I can offer only the excuse that my long sojourn in Purilia had habituated me to a mode of conduct which, a year earlier, would have struck me as indefensibly arbitrary and unreasonable. And, to my shame, I must confess that I was growing more and more conscious of fear, of a frantic desire to escape from that roseate, mellifluous atmosphere, and, even more, from the mysteries of Purilian marriage. And to those who would condemn me I can but say that no one who has not been in my situation can possibly understand the force of the impulse which now possessed me.

In any case, I was soon deep in the consideration of ways and means for the realization of my mad project. And, when the dawn came (with its customary panoramic effects and its routine enlargement of birds and the young of domestic animals), I crept softly out of the cottage, and repaired to the barn which housed the Cellula.

I almost wept for joy when I saw the familiar craft – my one link with the human world, to which my thoughts were turning more and more eagerly. I examined the aeroplane hastily, fearful that some harm might have befallen it in my absence; but I was delighted to find everything sound and in good order. I spent an hour or more in going over the great ship with the utmost care: testing every vital link, oiling every movable part, and secretly replenishing the depleted supplies of water, oil, and fuel. Then, with great difficulty, I succeeded in wheeling the craft out of the shed and into the field upon which poor Johnson and I had made our descent. This done, I started the motor. All was in readiness now, for an immediate flight; and, as the little white church at which we were to be married lay only a few hundred yards from the field, I had every hope of putting my desperate plan into execution. (I knew well enough that the sight of the Cellula, so close at hand, with its motor running, would arouse no suspicion in the minds of Pansy or the others. Such unusual spectacles are too common in Purilia to merit any attention.)

My preparations completed, I returned to the house, where I found the bridal party in readiness. The ceremony was to be a triple one: Mrs Malone and the governor and

Mollie and Charlie having decided upon immediate marriage too. A rather surprising piece of news awaited me. I learned that I was to marry an heiress! A telegram had arrived that very morning, informing Pansy that her uncle had been found mysteriously stabbed through the heart with a paper knife, and that she had inherited his entire vast fortune. While this decease of a near relative cast something of a shadow upon the nuptials, I learned that the late millionaire had been a bit of a roué and a ne'er-do-well (the governor informing me, privately, that he had been not only a prominent club-man but a well-known man-about-town); so that his loss could not be greatly deplored.

We all set out, now, for the little white church, whose bell was tolling joyously in anticipation of the wedding. Pansy and Mollie looked very charming, indeed, in their elegant white bridal-dresses, silk shoes, and long lace veils, which contrasted oddly with the rusty black dress and faded bonnet of Mrs Malone and the grotesque finery of Jim. A little knot of villagers was gathered about the door of the church, the approach to which had been strewn with wild flowers by several little bare-legged girls, with long ringlets. All Nature seemed to rejoice in our happiness – especially the birds, which, despite the season, sang merrily. As for the roses, their autumnal profusion was something to make one marvel.

As we entered the church, I could not help observing, despite my preoccupation with my plans for abducting Pansy, how strangely in contrast to the small and insignificant exterior of the structure were the vast dimensions of its interior: eloquent testimony to the genius of Purilian architects.

We were greeted by the clergyman, a sober-faced man, with a tendency to baldness. All was in readiness for the ceremony, and Mrs Malone and the governor, who were to be united first, took their places before the officiating minister.

The ceremony was a simple one and soon ended. Then, as

the clergyman pronounced the elderly couple man and wife, a most bewildering and unbelievable phenomenon occurred. As Mrs Malone and the governor slowly turned to each other, their faces expressive of dignified happiness, I saw to my utter astonishment, that their enlarged features grew dimmer and dimmer. At first, I assumed that my eyes were failing me, but as I looked about, hastily, I discerned Pansy and all the others, as clearly as before. Only the newly wedded pair were fading from my view. And, as I turned my eyes to them again, their features had grown so faint as to be almost invisible. Another instant and, to my unutterable horror, they had faded completely from view!

I could not believe it. But there was no room for doubt: a moment ago they had been standing there, not ten feet from me, and now no trace of them was visible. I turned to the others, expecting to see my horror mirrored in them. But a new wonder awaited me. The faces of the clergyman, of Pansy, and of all the others reflected only supreme happiness.

Suddenly, a terrible misgiving seized me. Could this, I wondered, be the end of spiritual love? Was this the solution of the mystery? Was marriage in Purilia synonymous with extinction, and was this goal, attainable only by a long ordeal of privation, suffering, separation, perilous pursuits, and hair-breadth escapes, and regarded by all right-thinking Purilians as the summit of happiness, only to be won at the cost of the complete obliteration of the happy pair?

While I was still formulating this terrifying hypothesis, I became aware that Mollie and Charlie had now taken their places before the clergyman, and were already exchanging their vows. Fearful of the worst, I fastened my eyes upon them, scarcely daring to breathe, every muscle tense. Then, as the clergyman pronounced the coupling formula and the young lovers – husband and wife now – turned their adoring gaze upon each other, I saw their features, too, begin to wane. With fascinated horror, I watched them grow more and more tenuous and impalpable, until the last faint vestige had faded into nothingness and there remained not a single evidence of the existence of the pair who, but a few moments before, had appeared so substantial.

No doubt remained, now. My worst fears were confirmed. And in another moment I too should experience the same fate. I turned my horror-stricken eyes on Pansy. The girl's lovely face wore a look which I knew by now betokened ecstasy; to her the imminent event connoted only blissful fulfilment. I wanted to take her up in my arms, and carry her bodily to the waiting Cellula. But my muscles refused to obey my will. And, before I had time to shake off my paralysis, Pansy took me by the hand and drew me gently toward the spot where the clergyman stood in readiness.

Mechanically, I took my place and, scarcely knowing what I was doing, murmured the appropriate responses to the familiar ritual. But, as the brief ceremony drew to its rapid conclusion, an awareness of the imminence of a peril greater by far than any that I had survived dispelled my lethargy and roused me to action. With a great effort, I drew back and shouted: 'Stop!'

But it was too late. The clergyman had already pronounced us man and wife, and I saw Pansy's eyes brimming with tears of happiness, as she turned her face to mine. Then, slowly, her features began to fade. And terror suddenly swept over me as I felt that I, too, was beginning to fade! I tried to seize Pansy, in the hope that there was still time to carry her off. But already she was too insubstantial; nothing remained of the vibrant, pulsating girl but an evanescent wraith. And, in another moment, I too should be but a vanishing shadow!

Everything deserted me now but the animal's desire for self-preservation. With a last great effort of the will, I wrenched myself free from that place of oblivion, and fled incontinently. With a speed that only impending obliteration could have lent me, I dashed up the aisle of the church and out into the road. One last terrified glance over my shoulder, as I sped through the door, revealed the last faint traces of

Pansy's beautiful features, the ghost of a beatific smile still upon them. Then, forgetting love and honour and manliness, and bent only upon escaping that dreadful vaporous annihilation, I ran across the fields to where the Cellula stood, its engine throbbing rhythmically.

Close at my heels followed the clergyman and all the attendants at the wedding, howling with rage and pelting me with missiles. To them, I was a blasphemer, an iconoclast. I had violated the most ancient and inflexible of Purilian laws and profaned the most sacred of Purilian mysteries.

I managed to reach the Cellula, climb into the cockpit and close the door, despite the hands that sought to restrain me. A pull of the lever, a brief quiver, and my ever-dependable craft began to move. Then with increasing speed I raced across the field, scattering in every direction the furious mob, and safe now from its missiles and its imprecations.

Soon, I began to mount and, before long, I could distinguish nothing beneath me, but a patchwork of field and forest and stream. The roaring of the motor shut out all other sound; and I experienced a sense of indescribable relief as, for the first time in many months, no note of that incessant, enveloping Purilian harmony penetrated my auditory apparatus.

On and on I plunged, through masses of pink cloud, which obscured completely now the land beneath. Then, as the pinkish vapour began to grow thinner, I closed the ventilators and adjusted my oxygen mask. Slowly and cautiously, I inhaled the gas. The first breath was like a draft of some exhilarating intoxicant. And, as my lungs filled with the pure, life-sustaining element, my aching head cleared, my eyes grew sharper, and I felt relief from that faint, persistent nausea which had plagued all my days in Purilia.

My speeding vehicle soon passed beyond the Purilian atmosphere; and, alone, I rode the immense void. Sorrow and joy fought for the possession of my being. Johnson, my dear comrade, was dead — the victim of a trivial and avoidable accident — and him I should mourn, to the end of my days. Pansy had faded into nothingness. But even in my grief, I reflected, that she, at least, had fulfilled her destiny — that for her this vaporous disintegration was the only conceivable end. And I saw, now, clearly that even had my abortive attempt at abduction been successful the ultimate result could not have been other than tragic. For a creature as fragile, as delicate, and as immaculate as Pansy could not long have survived the rigorous realities of our earth. Subjected no longer to the rosy light and the drugging harmonies, I knew now that she had worn but the semblance of flesh and blood. Actually, she had been no more than a lovely phantom, an insubstantial shadow, that had flickered alluringly, for a brief instant, before my bedazzled eyes.

I was soaring through blackness now. By straining my eyes, I could see, immeasurably distant, the last sign of Purilia: a faint and negligible pink smudge, in the black immensity of interstellar space. Then it faded completely; and I turned my eager eyes to the luminous globe that hung below me like a welcoming beacon: the world of human beings.

*The following pages
give details of other recent
Penguin Fiction*

AMERICAN FICTION

The Grapes of Wrath
JOHN STEINBECK

The striking and terrible story of a 'squatter' community driven from its bit of land in Oklahoma by the implacable march of industrial progress. (833)**　　　　　　　　3s 6d

Sanctuary
WILLIAM FAULKNER

An impressionist novel of character and violence, poignant and logical in method. It is the most famous of many books by the 1949 winner of the Nobel Prize for Literature. (899)**　　2s

Main Street
SINCLAIR LEWIS

An exuberant story of various people who live in a typical Middle-west town of the U.S.A. (790)**　　　　　　　3s 6d

H. M. Pulham Esquire
JOHN P. MARQUAND

The tragedy of an American educated as a gentleman and brought up in an already changing world. (798)**　　　2s 6d

Fombombo
T. S. STRIBLING

The adventures of a North American salesman with a revolutionary leader in Venezuela, described in a lightly satirical manner. (854)　　　　　　　　　　　　　　2s

Serenade
JAMES M. CAIN

James M. Cain belongs to the school of Ernest Hemingway and William Faulkner. He writes of violence, his themes are startling, and his style swift and abrupt. (902)**　　　　　2s

**NOT FOR SALE IN THE U.S.A. OR CANADA

FAST-MOVING THRILLERS

Erle Stanley Gardner has made a Penguin reputation in a very short time. The first of his books to appear in the series was *The Case of the Black-Eyed Blonde*, published in 1952. Since then, four others have followed it, and five more were published simultaneously at the beginning of this year. They are clever, fast-moving mystery stories, most of them featuring Perry Mason, the lawyer-detective of Los Angeles, whose cases often end with a brilliant courtroom cross-examination. The following are now available:

'A fine combination of the very intricate and the very dramatic into a clear story that keeps one reading from Chapter One to the end.' – *Morning Post*

'If you want a more satisfactory "thriller" of this particular kind you are likely to wait a long time.' – *Evening News*

'Perry Mason triumphs all along the line.' – *Punch*

2s each

READY SOON

The Case of the Abominable Snowman
NICHOLAS BLAKE
973

This book has to do with a snowman built on the lawn outside a house, with murder, with various remarkable people, and some intricate police work. Like all Nicholas Blake's books it tells a good story with art and distinction, and is superbly constructed.*

Love Lies Bleeding
EDMUND CRISPIN
974

Strange happenings occur in two schools close together. A girl of sixteen disappears from one and two masters are shot at the other. This is the first of Edmund Crispin's well-known detective stories to appear in Penguins.**

The Floating Dutchman
NICOLAS BENTLEY
975

A story of crisp, swift action and unfailing suspense. The setting is London – the London of the smaller, less reputable night clubs, one of which is run for strictly criminal purposes by a hero of the last war and his murderous assistant.*

Death of a Doll
HILDA LAWRENCE
977

A Home for Working Girls has had five years of uneventful existence until Ruth Miller arrives – a few hours later she is found dead in the courtyard. One small incident in her life brings to light enough (which the police hadn't even thought of) to pin the murder on the culprit. By the author of *Duet of Death*. (886)**

2s each

*NOT FOR SALE IN THE U.S.A.

**NOT FOR SALE IN THE U.S.A. OR CANADA

EVELYN WAUGH

In 1951 Evelyn Waugh joined those authors – including Bernard Shaw, H. G. Wells, and D. H. Lawrence – who have had ten of their books published simultaneously as Penguins.

This *enfant terrible* of English letters became a best-seller with the publication in 1928 of his first novel, *Decline and Fall*. Many of the characters in that masterpiece of derision reappear in the subsequent novels, which, culminating in *Put Out More Flags*, present a satirical and entertaining picture of English leisured society during the thirties. The selection also includes *Scott-King's Modern Europe* (together with *Work Suspended*, a novel interrupted by the war – hence the title – and a group of short stories), a satirical picture of life in a modern totalitarian state, and *The Loved One*, an account of the burial practices in southern California, which has had a *succès d'estime et de scandale* in two continents. More recently his *Life of Edmund Campion*, the famous Jesuit scholar and missionary whose martyrdom disfigured the reign of Elizabeth I, has joined the list. Titles available are: